BOOK THREE OF
THE DARK MATTER SERIES

SHADOW REALM

Shadow Realm is a work of fiction. The characters, incidents, and dialogue are drawn from the author's imagination and are not to be construed as real. Any resemblance to actual events or persons, living or dead, is entirely coincidental.

Copyright © 2019 by Clayton Smith

All rights reserved. Except as permitted under the U.S. Copyright Act of 1976, no part of this publication may be reproduced or used in any manner whatsoever without the express written permission of the publisher except for the use of brief quotations in a book review.

Printed in the United States of America

First Printing, 2019

ISBN 978-1-945747-06-9

Cover art and design by Steven Luna

For Dustin.
I think you would have liked this series.

BOOK THREE OF
THE DARK MATTER SERIES

SHADOW REALM

CLAYTON SMITH

CHAPTER 1

Simon woke up in a strange and terrifying place.

He had gone to sleep in his own bed—he was certain of that. He had fallen asleep under his own covers, in his own room, in the two-bedroom apartment he shared with Virgil, in the leaky old building on Wayward Street, where everything was nice and normal and familiar.

But he woke up somewhere altogether different.

The world in which he found himself was so wholly alien to his normal environment that he had trouble even comprehending what his eyes were showing him. He appeared to be sitting on a black, rubbery surface with a pebble-like texture, not too dissimilar from the spongy surface that was used for playgrounds now instead of gravel and dirt. The sky above was dark, a pitch black night sky with no stars, but it was also layered with flashes and swirls of color and light. It was like the videos he had seen of the Northern Lights, if there were ten different sets of Northern Lights, all in variegated colors, some green-to-blue, some purple-to-red, some yellow-to-orange, all laid over each other like layers of a cake, all flashing and swirling at the same time.

But the thick, black darkness above was present, and pressing...almost suffocating.

There were things that looked like trees sticking up from the ground, if trees were made of gigantic toothpicks glued together at all the wrong angles and painted dishwater-gray. The horizon stretched on, forever and ever, in all directions, and Simon had the distinct sense that he could see so far into the distance that if he had the right binoculars, he would actually be able to see himself at the far end of his vision.

Also, the entire world appeared to be sideways.

It didn't *look* sideways to Simon, because he was sitting up, and the ground was beneath him, and the sky was above him, but something about the gravity felt all wrong. It felt as if it wanted to pull him forward, and if he got up off his seat, he would plummet through the air, straight ahead, dragging his feet along the rubbery black floor.

"What...is this?" he said aloud. His voice sounded deadened and muted in the air, as though he were speaking into a thick wad of cotton. He lifted his right hand and tried to summon energy into his fist, so he would be ready to defend himself if he had to be. But the energy didn't respond.

He had no magic in this place.

"Hello!" he called out, and his voice fell flat as soon as the sound left his lips. He felt as if he could see the words falling down onto the ground and rolling away.

"Okay," he said quietly, turning around and seeing nothing but rubbery ground, flashing sky, and pale trees in every direction. "This has *got* to be a dream."

Just then, there was a sharp *SNAP-SNAP-SNAP* as the ground began to pop all around him, bursting like blisters and erupting with a thick, red goo. Simon cried out and leapt to his feet, precariously balancing himself against the weird push-pull of sideways gravity, and backed quickly away from the deteriorating rubber floor. The pops spread out in all directions as he backpedaled, and soon the whole world looked like a poorly-choreographed fountain show, with brilliant red streams arcing up from the floor in disastrous syncopation and streaming back down to the ground, splashing and coating what remained of the black floor with a sticky, bright-red sheen.

Simon turned and ran, trying to put distance between himself and the red fountains, but they spread more quickly than he could move, and soon the entire landscape, from one horizon to the other, was dotted with oozing red spray. Simon danced out of the way as two holes popped open beneath his feet; he stumbled to the side and slipped in a bit of the red muck. He fell onto his back with a low groan as the wind was knocked from his lungs. The goop was sticky, and he couldn't peel his arms off of it, or his legs, or the small of his back when he tried to kick himself up. He was a human fly stuck to a planet-sized piece of disgusting red flypaper, and as the fountains continued to spew their liquid, the level of the muck rose higher and higher, up over his hands, then over his legs, then up to his ears. Soon it would cover him completely, and he would drown in two feet of sticky red glop.

"Virgil," he gasped, his voice hoarse and muffled. "Help..."

Suddenly, something appeared in the swirling, flashing night. It started out small, hovering between the layers of sky, but it grew larger as it moved downward, approaching the surface of the planet. From far away, it looked like a piece of dark dandelion fluff floating in the air, with soft edges and a hazy center. As it floated lower to the ground, he realized that it was a small cyclone, grayish-blue in color, spinning and spinning and spinning at a dizzying pace, but in a surprisingly controlled manner.

It lowered itself toward Simon, and the closer it got, the slower the advance of the red goop became. By the time the cyclone was hovering thirty feet above the ground, the ocean of red was actually receding, as if it were being pushed back down the drain by the oncoming tornado.

The cyclone got closer and closer, finally coming to a stop just a few feet above Simon's prostrate body. And then, Simon heard it speak.

Light is the maker and the master of shadow.

Simon furrowed his brow. "What?" he said.

Light is the maker and the master of shadow, the cyclone repeated.

"Oh," Simon said, thoroughly confused. Most of his dreams these days were stress dreams that featured a sudden inability to read words in a grimoire or to remember to wear pants outside. He had an occasionally-recurring nightmare about his sister Laura clawing her way up out of a storm sewer. But he had never dreamt anything as weird as this.

"Okay," he said. The cyclone hovered there above him, not moving, and not saying anything more. Simon just lay there awkwardly for a few seconds before adding, "Thanks."

You're welcome, the cyclone said. Then it drifted back up into the sky and disappeared in the swirl of sky-light colors.

As soon as it was gone, the red goo returned with a fury, flooding the world around him, rising up like a tidal wave, drowning him in its thick wetness, and crashing down on him like a fist.

CHAPTER 2

Simon woke up with a gasp.

"I didn't hit you!" Virgil cried, jerking away from the edge of Simon's bed and tossing the plunger he was holding over his shoulder. "You woke up on your own!"

Simon blinked. He looked around the room. He blinked again. "What?"

"What? Nothing," Virgil said, looking up at the ceiling and trying his best to look casual. "You woke up on your own. Not because I hit you with a plunger."

Simon shook his head hard, trying to dislodge the last remnants of the dream from his mind. He squinted up at Virgil, who was barely distinguishable in the watery pre-dawn light. "You hit me with a plunger?"

"No. Don't you listen? I *didn't* hit you with a plunger." He relaxed a little, letting his shoulders slump. He picked up the plunger and gave it a twirl between his fingers. "I was *about* to hit you with a plunger, though."

"Why?" Simon asked.

"Because I thought it would wake you up."

"Why?" he repeated.

"Because I don't know about you, but if my roommate hit me in the face with a used plunger, I would wake up *instantly*." Virgil rubbed his jaw for a second, then he added, "My next move would probably be to throw my roommate out the window. So I guess it's good for both of us that you woke up on your own."

Simon threw up his hands, exasperated. "No, I mean why did you try to wake me up in the first place?!"

"Oh." Virgil hefted the plunger onto his shoulder and walked over to Simon's bedroom door. He pulled it open and gestured out to the kitchen. "'Cause of that."

Simon's room was directly across the hall from the kitchen. The lights were on in there, and he had to shield his eyes against the glare until they adjusted. When he could finally see, he rubbed the sleep from his eyes and peered out.

There were dirty glasses on the counter, dirty bowls on the table, and dirty plates on the island.

They were all hovering three inches in the air and spinning like tops.

Simon leapt out of bed with a cry of surprise. He gestured wildly out at the spinning dishes, then he gestured wildly back at Virgil. Then back out toward the dishes, then back toward Virgil. "What is happening?!" he finally yelled.

"I don't know!" Virgil yelled back. He hopped up and down anxiously and said, "It freaked me out, then I calmed down about it, and now you're making me freaked out again!"

"Why are the plates spinning, Virgil?!"

"I don't know, Simon!" Virgil shouted, pulling at his own hair in frustration. A streak of silver tufted up between his fingers, woven in against the darker brown. "I woke up to go to the bathroom, I was washing my hands, I looked up, and the toothbrushes are going all Tasmanian Devil!" He whirled his finger frantically through the air, in case Simon needed a visual aid. "Then I went out to the living room, and Alexa's just out there, pfffffft!" He made a helicopter noise with his lips and did another finger twirl to mimic the supernatural movement of their smart speaker. "Her cord's whipping around, she almost took my head off! Then I go into the kitchen, and *that's* happening," he said, pointing out the door with the plunger. "And I come in here, and you're sound asleep, and you won't wake up, and I'm screaming in your face, and you won't wake up, and I'm like, 'Well, Simon might actually be dead,' and there was only one way to know for sure, so I went back to the bathroom, grabbed the plunger, and I'm telling you, I'm glad I didn't have to hit you with it, but I was standing here trying to figure out if I should swing it like a bat or just straight-up plunge on your face, and I had pretty much decided to bash you in the head, and then you woke up, and Simon, *what is going on?!*"

"I don't know!" Simon shouted, rubbing his temples. "Give me a second to think, I just woke up!"

The plates and bowls and glasses suddenly lost momentum. They slowed down, wobbling in the air, coming to a stop altogether…then they came crashing down, shattering on the counter, the table, and the island, exploding on impact, and sending shards of glass sprinkling across the room.

"I think we might have a poltergeist," Virgil said quietly.

Simon grunted. "We're not that lucky," he replied. He turned on his bedroom lamp and pulled on his sneakers before stepping out into the kitchen, crunching carefully over the shattered glass. He dug the broom and dustpan out of the closet and set to work sweeping up the shards.

After a few minutes, he looked up at Vigil expectantly. "You going to help?" he asked, raising an eyebrow.

"I *want* to," Virgil said, "it's just that I'm barefoot." He lifted up one foot to prove to Simon that it was, in fact, bare. "My shoes are in my room, way down the hall."

Simon shook his head and muttered something under his breath.

"I hope whatever mean-spirited thing you just said was about the magic, spinning dishes and not about me," Virgil called from Simon's room.

"It was about both of you," Simon grumbled, sweeping the glass into the dustpan. He straightened up, leaned on the broom, and sighed. "It's just…between the Refracticore, and the Shadow Lord, and the backwards reflections in the Dixie Diner bathroom last Thursday, and now spinning plates and toothbrushes…there's a lot happening all of a sudden."

"'Backwards' is not the right word for those reflections," Virgil said as he remembered the shock at seeing the back of himself in the mirror. A shudder vibrated through his entire body. "I will never un-see that."

Simon dumped the broken glass into the trash can and blew air through his lips, sounding utterly exhausted. "I know it's only been, like, a week," he said, "but we can't keep facing these things, just us. We need help. We need Llewyn. We need him back."

"Wait," Virgil said, furrowing his brow. "What are you saying?"

Simon sighed. "I'm saying, Virgil, that I think it's time to let Morgan le Fay out of the box."

CHAPTER 3

"Do you think she's going to be mad that we left her in there so long?"

Virgil, Simon, and Abby all stood in Llewyn's dungeon room and stared uneasily down at the locked and sealed coffin before them.

Abby shrugged. "Judging by the look of the chains and the wax, I'd say she's already been in there for a couple hundred years, at least. I'm not sure a few more days is going to be what pushes her over the edge."

Virgil considered this. "Huh," he said. "Well in that case, do we think she's going to be mad that we as a *human race* left her in there so long?"

Abby tapped her lips. "That does seem likely," she decided. "Great."

Three days after Abby had summoned her, they had moved the legendary Arthurian sorceress to the basement of Llewyn's mansion, to a dungeon room that none of them had known existed until they went searching through all the open, non-frozen doors in order to find a safe place to store her. None of them exactly relished the idea of putting their hands on the box and lifting it up, much less carrying it a few hundred yards through the mansion and down a deep, deep flight of winding stone steps, but they couldn't bear to leave the coffin sitting in the hallway next to Llewyn's frozen form. They didn't want to see it every time they came into the hall, and as far as any of them knew, a box containing a powerful sorceress could explode or combust or become sentient or any number of things, and they reasoned that it was best for Llewyn if they moved her to a safe distance. So together, they had gathered up their courage, held their breath, grabbed the rickety coffin, and hauled the most powerful and dangerous sorceress in history down into the wizard's dungeon.

They had only dropped her four times.

"She's probably also not going to like the fact that we kept her prisoner in an underground torture cell," Simon pointed out, walking around the small room and running his hands along the cold, wet stone wall. Most of the stones were splotched white with niter, and when the torches set into the wall flamed to life—which happened of its own accord every time they approached—the entire room gave off an eerie, ghostly glow. The far wall was inset with chains and manacles that were properly positioned to secure two arms and two legs. The room could be barred with a heavy iron door, and the only toilet to speak of was a narrow grate set into the center of the floor.

They avoided that grate as much as possible.

"According to the stories, she's spent a good portion of her life in dungeons worse than this one," Abby pointed out.

"Maybe that'll work in our favor," Virgil suggested. "Maybe it'll feel homey."

"Yeah." Simon kicked over a small pile of rubble in the corner of the room, and a mummified rat tumbled out from beneath it. Simon blenched. "Real homey."

"If she's going to be mad about anything, it's going to be the fact that we dropped her on the way down here," Abby decided.

"Are we *sure* we want to do this?" Virgil asked. "We don't want to keep looking for a different way to thaw out old frostybeard? Or maybe just pack up and move to Wyoming, and never come back?"

"We've spent enough time looking for other ways to save Llewyn," Simon said with a note of finality. "We're just stalling.

If there were a better way, he would have told us. It's time to get him back."

"All right," Virgil said, raising his hands in defeat. "It's just that I've been reading a lot about Morgaine on Reddit lately, and—"

"We're letting her out!" Simon said.

Virgil looked at him curiously. But eventually, he nodded. "All right. Abby?"

"Let's do it," she said. "I'm not exactly thrilled about setting the world's most powerful sorceress free after someone took the time to bind her so well, and I think there's a decent chance she slaughters all three of us within half a second of escaping, but hey. It's our best and only option."

"Great," Virgil said miserably. "Well, then, what are we waiting for?" He clapped his hands and rubbed them together. "Let's get this party started."

The three of them cautiously approached the coffin. The box was definitely heavy enough to be holding a person inside, but Morgaine hadn't made a sound. It had crossed Simon's mind more than once that perhaps she wasn't even in there, despite the fact that her name was scrawled into the ancient wood. Part of him hoped the box was empty. But the greater part of him needed Llewyn, and he knew that she was the only hope of bringing him back. "Okay," he said, taking a deep breath. "Let's do it."

He extended his right hand toward the box, opening his palm over one of the heavy iron padlocks. He charged up his hand, said, "Here goes nothing," and shot a kinesthetic blast at the lock.

The bright orange light collided with the metal, bounced off, and ricocheted across the room, nearly taking off Virgil's head.

"*Whoa!*" Virgil screamed, falling backward and landing hard on his seat. "*Not okay!*"

"Huh," Simon said, looking down quizzically at his hand. He glanced over at the padlock, which looked completely untouched by the powerful magic blast. "Well, that didn't work."

"You think?!" Virgil cried. He pushed himself back up to his feet and brushed off his jeans. He gave Simon a look of warning. "*Not* okay," he said again.

"There's a pretty good chance the locks are immune to magic," Abby said. She bent down and inspected the chains, running her hand over the metal links, which were warm to the touch, despite the damp chill of the dungeon. "Magic might not do the trick."

"Now she tells us," Virgil mumbled, elbowing Simon in the ribs. Simon ignored him.

"Makes sense that you wouldn't want to lock a powerful sorcerer in a box that can be opened by sorcery," Simon agreed. "Does Llewyn have an axe or something? Or a shovel, or bolt cutters, or…I don't know, any sort of tool we can use to cut through the chains?" He shot Virgil a glare. "Maybe a toilet plunger?"

"I said I didn't hit you with it!" Virgil cried.

Abby shook her head as she inspected the wax along the seams of the coffin, picking at it with her nails. "I clearly missed something that I don't think I want to be brought up to speed on," she said. She stood up and brushed off her hands. "I'm not sure about an axe, but I know where we can get a key."

"Where?" Simon asked. Abby looked at him meaningfully, arching an eyebrow and planting her hands on her hips. "Oh!" Simon said. "You mean *my* key? My curiocus key?"

"It's opened every lock you've tried it in so far, right?"

"Well, yeah," Simon replied, his face suddenly set in a frown. "But…"

"Hold on," Virgil interrupted, stepping between Simon and Abby. "You just said magic won't work."

Abby adjusted her glasses on her nose. "Magic spells clearly don't," she mused, "but it's possible that artifacts may. I imagine it might depend whether the key is made of magic, or if it's a non-magical item that had magic bestowed upon it." Both she and Virgil turned to look at Simon. "Well?"

"What? How am I supposed to know?" Simon asked, taking a few steps back to put some physical distance between himself and the question. "I just put my hands on a flower and got a magic key."

"It's worth a shot," Abby shrugged.

Simon furrowed his brow. "Yeah, but—"

"Yeah, get the key," Virgil urged.

"Okay, it's just—"

Abby eyed him suspiciously. "Is there some reason you don't want to try the key?"

"Well, aside from being a little nervous about the fact that it would release an evil sorceress into the world, everyone seems to be forgetting that there's a Refracticore inside my psychic vault that might shrivel me to death when I open the door," Simon pointed out.

Abby blinked. "Oh, that," she said.

"Yes, Abby, *that*," Simon retorted, crossing his arms. "Call me crazy, but I don't want to be a mummy."

"It's not so bad," Virgil chimed in. He smiled as he massaged his temples with the tips of his fingers. "My knees crack when I walk, but the wrinkles make me look smart."

"They make you look old," Simon countered.

Virgil frowned. "Well, that's just hurtful," he said.

"Sorry." Simon patted his friend encouragingly on the shoulder. "It makes you look good old, not bad old. Really." He turned back to the coffin and bit his lip in nervous thought as he considered the locks. "I just don't know what the Refracticore will do. It's been locked up in there for a week and a half, and it might be ready to blow."

"Only one way to find out," Abby said. She took Simon's hand in her own, giving it a squeeze through her glove. "I promise, even if it turns you old and gray, we'll go on that redo date." She winked.

Simon suddenly burned red from the bottom of his chin to the tips of his ears. "That's not—I don't—I—that wasn't—" he stammered.

Abby laughed, then she pushed herself up on the tips of her toes and kissed him on the cheek. "Everything's going to be great," she smiled.

The way she said it, Simon couldn't help but believe her.

"Okay," he nodded, giving her hand a squeeze, then stepping back to give himself some room. "Okay." He shook out his hands, cracked his neck, and exhaled. "Here we go."

He closed his eyes and pictured his psychic vault, a massive, circular thing with a keypad set into the door. In his imagination, he reached out and pressed the code, 6-0-6-2-1. The lock slid back with a hydraulic hiss, and Simon gripped the handle. *Here goes nothing*, he thought.

In his mind, he pictured himself pushing down on the handle and cracking open the door. He put his eye to the seam and slowly opened the vault.

There was a thunderous *CRACK!* as the Refracticore shot out a massive bolt of energy that hummed and fizzled as it rocketed at Simon's head.

"Whoa!" Simon screamed, dropping down in his imagination as the explosion blasted past his face. He opened his eyes, and it was exactly the wrong instant to do that; he was pulled back into the real world, and the Refracticore's blast came with him. It appeared in the air like a flash of lightning, streaking across the dungeon and zapping Virgil squarely in the chest.

Virgil screamed as the energy bolt pierced him, lodging deep in his sternum, buzzing and sparking with the transfer of energy. Then, just as suddenly as it had appeared, it evaporated, leaving Virgil with a burn hole in the center of his hoodie and a red heat mark on his chest.

Virgil fell to the floor, flapping his arms and beating his chest with his hand, as if trying to put out a fire that didn't exist. He kicked his feet and pushed himself back across the floor in a panic, coming to a stop against the far wall. He scrabbled up the wall, feeling his chest for permanent damage. "Am I dead?! Am I dead?!" he shrieked, pushing himself to his feet. "Am I— ohh," he said, his tone suddenly softening. He bounced a few times, flexing his knees without a single crack or pop. "Oh! It was *youth* energy!" he said happily. He beamed as he jogged in place for a few steps, lifting his knees up to his chest. "I feel so much better!"

Simon exhaled with relief. He placed a hand over his heart, trying to calm himself down. "Thank goodness," he said.

"How do I look?" Virgil asked. "Is my hair brown again?"

"*Some* of it is," Abby said, reaching up and picking through his locks. "That silver streak is holding on strong, though."

Virgil shrugged. "Eh, well. I'll just keep looking distinguished, I guess." He touched the skin around his eyes; it felt smooth and soft again. "Not bad, not bad! Thanks, Simon!"

"Don't mention it." Simon hauled himself back to his feet. He closed his eyes again and returned to his vault. The door was hanging open, and he peered inside cautiously, but the Refracticore had expelled its last bit of pent-up energy, and it now sat on the floor of the vault, a cold, lifeless, dull purple stone.

Simon stepped inside the vault, carefully picked up the Refracticore, and placed it on the shelf a few yards away from the door. "Stay," he said, as if it were some sort of misbehaving pet. Then he turned and headed back out of the vault, grabbing his key from its perch next to the door on the way. He closed the door, locked the keypad, and opened his eyes.

The antique key was now in his palm.

He hadn't had reason to retrieve the mystical key since the Asag adventure at Mrs. Grunberg's house a few months earlier, and Simon was surprised at how comforting it was to hold the key in his hand. The weight of it felt familiar and powerful, and when he held it between his fingers, it became almost a natural extension of his hand, as if it truly belonged there.

"You're going to help me save the world," he said quietly to the key.

Virgil inclined his head toward Simon. "What'd you say?" he asked.

Simon's cheeks burned even brighter red. "Nothing," he said quickly. He didn't know why he'd said that. He blinked and shook his head, clearing away whatever spell the key seemed to have cast on him. Then he looked at Abby and Virgil. "Everybody ready?" he asked. They nodded. Simon took a deep breath and placed one hand on the coffin lid. The wood felt warm against his skin, and he thought he could feel it vibrating in anticipation.

He moved his hand along the rough plank, over the wax-sealed edge, and down to the first of three locks. He held his breath as he slipped the key into the hole.

It was a perfect fit.

He turned the key, and the lock mechanism moved as smoothly as if it had just been oiled. There was a loud click, and the lock popped open.

Everybody froze, waiting for something to happen...but nothing did. Abby nodded encouragingly, so Simon unhooked the lock and loosened the chain. Then he moved onto the second lock, a smaller, rusty thing of plated metal. His curiocus key unlocked that one, too, and he unwound the second chain from the box.

Now there was only one chain remaining. It was the biggest of the three, with heavy iron links, each of which was bigger than Simon's thumb. The padlock was the size of a saucer, made of solid iron coated with black enamel. Simon glanced nervously at his friends. "This is it," he said.

Virgil blew air through his lips, which was about as much encouragement he could manage, under the circumstances. "Do it," Abby said, and she sounded much more resolute than she looked.

"Okay," Simon said, exhaling loudly. "Here's hoping she doesn't slaughter us all."

He slipped the key into the lock and set the sorceress free.

CHAPTER 4

Morgaine exploded through the coffin, shattering the wood and the chains with a deafening *BANG!* and sending slivers of iron and timber in every direction. The three mortals in the room cried out in alarm and shielded their faces with their arms, and splinters of wood and metal lodged in their skin like pins in a cushion. They were knocked backward the by force of the explosion, and all three slammed against the stone wall, then slumped to the floor, dazed and in pain.

Virgil peered up between his trembling hands. The dark sorceress of legend stood before them, terrible in her fury, furious in her beauty. She was tall and powerful, wearing a long, sapphire-blue dress that hugged her curves and tapered at her waist before flowing down to the floor. There was a split in the side that ran from the hem all the way up to her thigh, and the sleeves came down past her wrists, narrowing down into triangles that covered the backs of her hands, looped over her middle fingers, and crossed back up her palms, rejoining the full sleeve on the undersides of her forearms. Her dark-brown hair was long and untamed, framing her oval face like a lion's mane. Her lips were full and blood-red, and the calm evenness of them betrayed the anger that flared in her dark violet eyes, rimmed with glowing flecks of silver.

"Why did you wake me?" she demanded. Her words lilted with a lyrical English accent.

"Wake you?" Virgil asked, the words coming out slow and thick, like verbal molasses. "We…freed you."

The sorceress stepped forward, fire burning in her eyes. She crouched down to Virgil's level and took his chin in her palm. Her fingers smelled of brimstone. "Morgaine of the Fay does not need a pre-pubescent boy to free her. She bides her time and releases herself when she wills it."

Virgil stared at her with fear, his insides turning to water under her withering gaze. "I'm not pre-pubescent," was all he could think to say.

Morgaine straightened up to her full height, scowling down at them. She did a broad turn and took in the surroundings: the hanging chains, the dripping stones, and the foul grate in the center of the room. She wrinkled her nose, shook her head, and said, "Ridiculous." She crossed her arms in front of her chest, then she threw them wide, transforming into a cloud of sapphire-blue vapor. The mist slipped through the open dungeon door and disappeared up the cold and winding stairwell.

The three lay there for several long minutes.

Finally, Abby cleared her throat. "On second thought," she said, "maybe we should have spent a little more time exploring other options."

CHAPTER 5

They picked wood and metal splinters from their arms as they trudged up the stairs back to the main floor of Llewyn's mansion.

"Llewyn knew what he was doing," Abby said as they climbed the steps, sounding like she was trying to convince herself as much as anybody. "He wouldn't have instructed us to summon her if she wasn't the right person for the job."

"Llewyn was on the literal edge of death when he left that message, and if the fever and disorientation you felt when you had the dark blade poison inside of you is any indication, he wasn't exactly in his right mind," Simon pointed out as he pried a particularly deep-set sliver of iron from the tender flesh below his wrist. "Ow."

Abby frowned down at her hands. Her palms still bore the black freckle-marks where Morilan's poison had seeped into her skin, and then back out of it when it returned to Llewyn. No amount of scrubbing seemed to be able to wear away the marks, and she was starting to wonder if her hands were permanently tattooed. "Even if she's the harbinger of the apocalypse, there's nothing to be done about it now. We brought her here, we set her free, and it's done. Now we just have to hope she plays by the rules."

Virgil snorted. "If there's one thing I know about Medieval witch-wizards, it's that they love playing by the rules," he said, panting from the effort of the climb.

Simon hitched an eyebrow in his direction. "You're an expert on Medieval witch-wizards now?" he said.

Virgil shrugged. "I figure *anyone* who was alive during the Middle Ages and who's still around now can't possibly have stayed alive by walking the straight and narrow path. I've seen *Game of Thrones*. I know about leprosy and sepsis."

"*Game of Thrones* doesn't take place during the Middle Ages," Abby pointed out.

"Then why are there so many dragons?" Virgil shot back.

Simon narrowed his eyes at his friend. "You know dragons weren't *actually* real, right?"

Virgil snorted. He tapped a finger against his temple. "That's what the dragons *want* you to think," he said.

Simon was hard at working trying to figure out how to pivot away from this particularly inane conversation when they turned a corner and found Morgaine circling the frozen form of Llewyn, scrutinizing him carefully, her eyes huge with surprise. "Is this man Llewyn Dughlasach of Moray?" she asked, incredulous.

"As opposed to Llewyn Dughlasach of suburban Pittsburgh?" Virgil murmured sarcastically.

Simon shot him a look.

"Sorry," Virgil whispered.

Abby stepped up and cleared her throat. "It is," she said, sounding much more calm than either Simon or Virgil felt. "The kinesthetic mage of the Seventh Order, last of the line of Highlands practitioners of True Magic, Llewyn of Moray."

"How has he come to this end?" Morgaine demanded. "Who cursed him thus?" She sized up the three of them, looking them slowly up and down. "Not you," she said dismissively.

"Hey..." Virgil protested.

Simon elbowed him in the ribs, and Virgil whimpered audibly.

"He froze himself," Abby said. "He put himself in stasis to stop a dark poison from entering his heart."

Morgaine set her lips into a hard line. She traced a finger along the icy surface of Llewyn's chest. "Morilan's dark blade has done its work, then," she said quietly. She stopped her finger when it reached the area in front of his sternum, then she spread her hand wide and pressed her entire palm against the cold surface. The ice beneath it turned invisible, the perfect clarity spreading several inches from her hand in every direction, until she could see through the thick frost down to his chest. She clicked her tongue as she examined the state of the wizard beneath the ice, at the poisoned black veins that crisscrossed his skin like a dark web, and the exposed wound in his chest that burned pink with infection.

For several long seconds, Morgaine considered Llewyn's frozen form. Then she removed her hand, and the ice lost its invisibility, obscuring his skin from their view in its blueish-white distortion once again.

"I suppose you want me to fix him," Morgaine scowled, turning to the other three and rubbing warmth back into her cold hand.

They looked at each other uneasily. "Well, I think—technically—Llewyn wants you to fix him," Simon said carefully, trying his best not to anger the sorceress.

"We, also, think that would be...good," Virgil added.

Morgaine considered this, crossing her arms, stepping back, and examining the entirety of the frozen wizard. "Why would I help him?" she asked, but not unkindly. She sounded as if she were deciding whether or not to engage in a simple business transaction.

"We honestly have no idea," Abby said. "We're just kind of following orders."

Morgaine snorted softly, lost deep within some secret memory. She circled the frozen wizard, considering him carefully. "So. The great Llewyn Dughlasach of Moray of the Highlands has been brought low by an upstart conjurer from the continent," she whispered, smiling as she said it. Then she addressed the three people in the hallway over her shoulder without breaking her gaze. "We have a history," she explained.

"We assumed," Simon muttered. He started clenching and unclenching his hands, and Virgil knew he was starting to lose his patience.

"I suppose I might help him," Morgaine decided, trailing back around to Llewyn's other side and tapping her lips thoughtfully. "In exchange for a favor."

"Uh, we sort of *did* you a favor by letting you out of the box," Virgil pointed out.

He was running out of patience, too.

"You distorted an inevitable timeline, unprompted," Morgaine corrected him, dismissing his notion with a simple wave of her hand. "That's not a favor; it's a cosmic detriment. I *should* demand a second favor for that fault as well." She lifted her arms above her head and pushed them toward the ceiling, purring like a kitten and enjoying the luxury of a stretch. "Still, I'm feeling particularly benevolent, so I'll trade your wizard's life for just one favor."

"What kind of favor?" Abby asked warily. She shot Simon a glance from the sides of her eyes that was meant as a warning against bestowing favors upon evil wizards.

Simon bit his lip in consternation. He was feeling a little out of his depth, and he didn't know what to do.

"A favor to be named," Morgaine said, pulling her arms gracefully through the air, testing out the open space around her. "A favor of unlimited degree. And at a time of my eventual choosing."

Simon exhaled and ruffled his hands through his short, blond hair. "What do you think?" he asked Abby.

"Agree to whatever, then have Llewyn blast her back to Merlin!" Virgil cut in with a sharp rasp.

Simon and Abby ignored him.

"It's a risk," Abby said, cocking her lips to one side in a way that made Simon's heart feel warm and weak. "A *big* risk. Being in debt to a sorcerer is incredibly dangerous. And when it's a sorcerer as powerful as Morgan le Fay..." she trailed off, letting her eyes wander to the supernatural force who hovered around their frozen friend. "It's a risk," she said again.

"But it's a bigger risk to keep Llewyn frozen," Simon said. "With him thawed, we have a better shot at handling whatever she can throw at us."

"That's true," Abby conceded. Then she turned and directed her next words to Morgaine. "When you bring him back, will you be able to remove the dark blade from his system? Completely?"

Morgaine laughed. "He wouldn't be back long if I didn't," she purred.

"That's not a yes," Virgil pointed out.

Morgaine smirked in his direction. "Not as dumb as you look," she said, sizing him up. "Yes; when I bring him back, he'll *stay* back. And that means the dark blade will be removed."

"I don't think we have a choice," Simon said, his voice wary and strained. "We'll trade you a favor for bringing Llewyn back. No questions asked. Just bring him back."

"Lovely," Morgaine laughed, clapping happily. "Prepare for your wizard to be saved." She waved her hands over her wrists, first one, then the other, and the fabric triangles that connected her hands to her sleeves disappeared. Her hands now freed, she pushed her sleeves up to her elbows and flexed her fingers, closing her eyes as a long-dormant power flowed through her and set the tips of her fingers glowing with a rosy red light. "I've changed my mind about our happenstance. In retrospect, I'm quite glad for the way you inserted yourself into the timeline of inevitability," she said with a wicked grin.

Then she turned back to the frozen form of the wizard, pressed her hand against the icy surface, and, with a bright red flash, shot a powerful magic through Llewyn, blasting him to bits, shattering him into a million pieces.

CHAPTER 6

"Llewyn!" Simon screamed.

He rushed forward, blinded by shock and anger, and dove at Morgaine, aiming to knock her away from the shattered wizard with his shoulder. But instead of connecting, he sailed right through her as she phased herself briefly out of existence, and he went sliding on his chest through the frozen shards of Llewyn. He scrambled to his knees, spreading his hands over the pieces and gathering them together into a pile. "Llewyn!" he shrieked again, pushing his hands together, gathering a couple handfuls of broken wizard.

He looked up at Morgaine with tears spilling over his cheeks. "What did you do?!" he demanded.

Morgaine frowned down at the young man. Then she turned to his two friends. "He seems upset," she said.

Virgil's face had drained to a pale white. "You…you killed Llewyn," he said, his voice hollow. He felt like he was going to be sick.

But Morgaine dismissed his words with a wave of her hands. "I didn't kill him," she insisted. "He's fine!" She gazed back over her shoulder and considered the scattering of frozen wizard pieces behind her. "More or less."

Simon gaped up at her, tears stinging his eyes. "He's not *fine!*" he shouted, scooping up a pile of ice shards and holding them up for her to see. "How can you say he's fine?! He's not fine!"

"I said more or less," she replied. She brushed the pieces of Llewyn from Simon's hand and pulled him up to his feet. "He's *going* to be fine. This is part of the process."

"What process?" Simon demanded, tearing himself away from Morgaine and stepping carefully out of the mess of wizard shards. "This isn't a *process*; Llewyn trusted you, and you blasted him into a million pieces!"

"Yes, there *are* many pieces—enough pieces that Morilan's poison has been rendered useless." She gestured to the floor with a sweeping arc of her hand, and Simon took a closer look at the shards of wizard beneath them. Interspersed between the bits of icy sorcerer were thin, frozen black slivers. The poison that had filled Llewyn's veins was now smashed and scattered along with the rest of the mage. "You'd be hard-pressed to find a practitioner of magic who could draw out the dark blade poison from Llewyn's veins from inside of his body," she explained. "It's a complex magic that won't readily bend to another's will. Drawing it out is practically impossible. But *break* the wizard's veins, scatter them to the floor, and the poison essentially separates itself."

Virgil scratched his head. He cleared his throat uncomfortably. "So you...broke Llewyn to draw out the poison?" he asked.

"Finally, someone has decided to pay attention," Morgaine replied.

"But...you also smashed him into bits," Virgil pointed out.

"For now, yes," Morgaine agreed, "and it *will* take some work to stitch him back together. Fortunately for you, and for him, I am Morganna of the Fae, and not some amateur boy-wizard." She looked meaningfully at Simon, who shrank back under her withering gaze.

Morgaine twirled her wrist, and the pieces of Llewyn began to swirl on the floor. Simon backed away as the frozen bits of wizard rose into the air, spinning in a lazy circle, moving like a cyclone in slow motion. Simon instantly flashed back in his mind to the dream of the night before, to the whirling tornado in the flashing sky, and the red wave that had swallowed him whole.

He gave his head a shake, to clear the memory.

He'd never had such a vivid dream.

Morgaine continued to swirl her wrist, and she moved down the hall, pushing the slowly-spinning pieces before her. "I'm going to mend him," she said. "To do that, I need complete concentration. Leave."

She disappeared down the ruined hall and through the open door, in search of a quiet place to work.

Simon, Virgil, and Abby all watched her go. "Well...bright side: today can't possibly get any weirder," Virgil said.

Abby checked her watch. "The lizard-monster herpetomorph is meeting us at the office in thirty minutes," she said.

Virgil rubbed his forehead. "Then again, I could be wrong," he sighed.

They trudged out of the mansion, leaving Morgaine to her work.

CHAPTER 7

"I don't know how it's possible, but this place looks even *more* depressing now," Virgil groaned.

The movers had finally gotten around to loading up and carting off the washers and dryers from the old laundromat, which Virgil had hoped would make the whole place feel a little bit more like an office...or, at the very least, a little bit less like a low-rent disaster zone. But the machines had been in place for so long that they had left behind rusty outlines on the linoleum, ugly, brownish squares that stained the floor like mechanical footprints. And now that the laundry machines were gone, the glare from the awful florescent lights bounced off of every tile, so that Virgil had to squint just to keep his head from splitting open in pain.

"Yeah," Simon admitted, "I didn't count on the rust stains. But come on, Virg! It's all going to come together! I mean, we've got the sign already, and that looks great!"

Virgil frowned. "Yeah...I've been meaning to talk to you about the sign..." he murmured.

The Dark Matter Investigations sign that Simon had paid for with some of his inheritance money had been officially installed the previous week. Simon hadn't stopped beaming with pride since it had gone up. Virgil, on the other hand, had spent the last week trying to figure out a tactful way to share his opinions.

"What, you don't like the sign?" Simon asked, his heart sinking.

Virgil grimaced, working hard to figure out the best way to put it. "It's not that I don't like it," he said slowly, piecing his critique together as he spoke. "It's just...I mean...why is it a *key?*"

The sign was a thick, die-cut aluminum monstrosity that was bigger than Virgil. It was so big that it took up the entire space above the office door, and the top edge of it poked up above the roof line. The aluminum sheet had been cut into the shape of an antique key, and beneath that were the words DARK MATTER INVESTIGATIONS. The key and the lettering had been mounted onto a weird metal bracket that the sign didn't cover completely, so the whole thing looked industrial and unfinished. Also, the bracket had LED lights running across the edges, so that at night, they could flick a switch, and the whole sign would be backlit with a soft white glow.

"You don't like the key?" Simon frowned.

"I don't understand *why* it's a key," Virgil countered. "Shouldn't it be, like, a magnifying glass, or a Sherlock Holmes hat, or a picture of Humphrey Bogart, or a Maltese falcon, or something?"

"We're not those kinds of investigators," Simon said, crossing his arms. "We're not film noir detectives."

"Well, we're not locksmiths, either," Virgil shot back.

"The key represents our ability to *unlock* your mystery!"

"It represents our *in*ability to *unlock* a good logo!"

"Well, I'm sorry, Virgil, I guess I just wasn't quite sure what kind of logo really screams 'two amateur wizards who fight demons and shadow lords with power blasts and Skee-Balls!'" Simon shouted, his voice dripping with sarcasm.

"You leave Gladys out of this!" Virgil cried.

"Hey. Drama queens," Abby called out, clapping her hands at them from the storeroom in the back, which served as her makeshift office. "Do you mind? I'm trying to keep Larry from turning into a lizard-monster." The herpetomorph poked his head around the doorway and gave them an awkward wave.

"Sorry, Abby, it's just that Simon asked what I think of the sign, so I have to tell him what I think of the sign. *I'm being a good friend,*" Virgil said, directing the last sentence toward Simon like a dagger.

"You're being completely unsupportive!" Simon retorted.

"Because you got us a sign that makes it look like we're a bank from 1904!"

"A key is a powerful symbol!" Simon insisted.

"You're a powerful blockhead!" Virgil shouted back.

"*Guys!*" Abby's voice pierced the room, cutting straight through them. Both men fell silent. "Simon obviously made the logo a key because he's insecure about the fact that his curiocus is a key and not an overtly powerful weapon like a solid wooden ball, now will you *stop?!*" She slammed the storeroom door so hard that it rattled in its frame.

They stared at the closed door with wide eyes.

"She can be really scary sometimes," Virgil whispered.

Simon sighed. Abby was a little blunt, but she also had a decent point. "I'm sorry I didn't let you help design the logo," he said. He rubbed his hand along the back of his head. "I guess what Abby said isn't...*totally* untrue."

Virgil smiled guiltily. "I'm sorry I made a big deal out of it," he said. "The sign is totally fine."

"Thanks," Simon said, sounding relieved.

"No one's going to see it anyway. We only have one client, and I keep forgetting to give out business cards."

Simon frowned again. "That's the spirit."

Virgil grabbed the remote control and turned on the old TV. The screen slowly came to life, the colors fading in to show two news anchors chatting from behind a desk. "Why is it *always* the news?" Virgil groaned. "Hasn't anyone in network TV heard about cartoons?" He flipped through the channels, but they only got reception from four local stations on the antiquated television set, and all four of them were showing the news.

Virgil sighed, flipped back to the first channel, and tossed the remote control down on the desk.

Abby and the herpetomorph emerged from the back room. She led him toward the front door, patting him consolingly on the shoulder. "You're doing great," she said encouragingly. "With enough time, we'll be able to build an empathetic semi-structural wall around the lizard inside you and keep him trapped. Like a feeling-energy net."

"Thank you," the herpetomorph said, his eyes glassy with gratitude. "You have no idea...I haven't had an episode in ten days, and I just..." He was so choked up that he didn't seem able to get out the words. "You just have no idea," he finally said again. He shook her gloved hand excitedly, gave the boys a wave, and bounced out the front door.

"How much is he paying, again?" Simon asked.

"It's not about the money; it's about helping someone," Abby said indignantly.

"Oh, so it's pro bono?" Virgil asked, raising an eyebrow knowingly.

Abby snorted. "Not even close. A hundred bucks per session."

"A hundred bucks a session?!" Virgil started. His mouth opened into a wide circle. "Wow. Maybe *I* should get into empathing..."

"Great," Simon said with a sigh. "So all we need is for him to have three sessions a day, and we can actually pay the rent on this place." He plopped down into his chair, leaning his forehead down onto the folding table he used for a desk. It was the only piece of furniture in the room aside from an old, musty recliner that he and Virgil had found next to the dumpster across the street and hauled inside earlier in the week.

The chair made the whole room smell like mold, and it had brought in a ton of bugs. But it *was* pretty comfortable to sit in.

"This place can't possibly cost that much," Virgil said sourly, looking around. "There are skid marks on the floor."

"Well, as much as I love where this conversation is heading, I have to get to my shift," Abby said.

"What shift?" Virgil asked, confused. "I thought Squeezy Cheez got destroyed by the Refracticore."

"*That* Squeezy Cheez got destroyed by the Refracticore. So I've been reassigned to the one across town, up in Meriwether Heights."

"Woof. That's a long drive," Virgil pointed out.

"No kidding," she said dryly. She grabbed her jacket from the back of Simon's chair and shrugged into it. "Oh, one more thing," she said, digging her phone out of her coat pocket. "Get together. We need a photo."

"Why?" Virgil asked, automatically smoothing down his hair, which was in its more-or-less-perpetual state of disarray.

"Because I want to run some Instagram ads. See if we can expand our clientele beyond Larry the herpetomorph."

"Larry is such a weird name," Virgil said, scrunching up his face in displeasure.

Abby ignored him. "Come on—up," she said to Simon, grabbing him gently by the collar and hauling his head up off the desk. "Everything's going to be fine. We're going to get more clients, we're going to make rent, and hey...didn't Llewyn give you a magic wallet?"

"He gave *me* a magic wallet," Virgil said. "But it hasn't filled itself up since he put himself into stasis. When he froze, so did our assets."

"Well, let's see if we can get some traction on some ads before Simon burns through all his drive-thru money. Get together," she said, waving at them with her phone.

"Should we take it in front of the sign?" Simon asked, standing up from the chair.

Abby grimaced. "Maybe let's leave the sign out of it for now," she suggested.

Simon and Virgil stood shoulder-to-shoulder, and they posed. Virgil beamed at the camera with a goofy smile, while Simon put on what he thought was a suitably business-forward face. "Simon, stop doing that with your mouth," Abby suggested.

"Doing what?"

"Whatever it is you're doing. Don't do it so much."

Simon sighed. "Let's just get this over with," he said.

Abby pressed the button, and the phone flashed. Virgil cried out in pain, stumbling dramatically backward, and Simon rubbed his eyes. "Whoops," Abby said, tapping on the screen and turning off the flash. "Sorry, sorry. One more." She took another photo, considered it, then nodded. "Close enough," she said.

"You say it in a way that fills me with inspiration," Simon said dryly.

Abby shrugged. "I'll run it through a filter." She grabbed her bag and tucked it under her arm, fishing out her keys and heading toward the door. "I'll see you tomorrow," she said. "Don't burn the place down while I'm gone."

"Hmm...that's a thought," Virgil said, tapping his lips thoughtfully as she walked outside. "If we burn this building to the ground, we'll have to get a new office."

He glanced sideways at Simon, looking for a reaction, but Simon wasn't paying attention.

He was focused completely on the television screen, his eyes wide with interest. He reached down and picked up the remote, turning up the volume. "Well," he said, walking closer to the screen, "*that's* not something you see every day."

CHAPTER 8

The local news had switched to one of their star reporters, a raven-haired woman with dark green eyes named Tracy Thornton. She was standing in front of an empty field that was ringed by a thick border of trees. A stone driveway stretched into the field behind her, leading to a huge, sprawling geometric pit dug into the ground. The edges were straight, and the corners were all right angles, as if someone had carefully dug a massive grid of overlapping squares and rectangles into a wide open field.

The hole in the ground looked like the footprint of an enormous, artfully-designed mansion.

"Thanks, Lisa," Tracy said into her microphone, holding unblinking eye contact with the camera. "I'm standing at the entrance to the Grimsley Estate, the ancestral home of the Grimsley family, who founded Templar back in the late-nineteenth century. The estate is still here, but as you can see behind me, Grimsley Manor itself is not. Neighbors awoke this morning, puzzled to see an empty hole in the ground instead of the 60,000-square-foot mansion that usually stands on the property. From the tops of its thirteen chimneys to the floors of the lowest sub-basement, the entire home has completely vanished without a trace."

Simon and Virgil stalked slowly closer to the television, mesmerized by what they were seeing. "How does an entire house just disappear?" Simon breathed.

"Especially a house that's the size of a small country," Virgil added.

The television became a split-screen, with the news anchor at the station desk taking up half of the space. "Tracy, was anyone inside the mansion when it disappeared?"

"Yes, Lisa," the reporter responded, "there's a full-time house staff employed at Grimsley Manor, including a butler, four maids, and several members of kitchen staff. All employees actually live in the house, and by all accounts, all of them were home last night when the manor disappeared. Now, Peter Grimsley III, the owner of Grimsley Manor, was *not* in the house; we're told that he's currently in Pittsburgh for business, and as you know, Mr. Grimsley has no spouse or children, so investigators believe that only the staff members were in the house when it vanished."

"And, Tracy, do the police have any leads on where the house might have gone?"

"No, they don't. The investigation is ongoing, of course, but the initial inspection revealed no evidence of a house ever having been here at all, except for the hole, and for the plumbing and electrical pipes left sticking out of the ground. The house, the garage, the foundation—everything is gone."

"Thanks, Tracy." The camera cut back to a full shot of both anchors sitting at the news desk. "This is just the latest in a string of strange incidents surrounding Peter Grimsley; early last month, Grimsley, who is widely known for his love of collecting, driving, and, most often, being driven in rare cars, was seen riding the Templar subway," Lisa said. "He caught the attention of several commuters when it became clear that he didn't know how to purchase or use a transit card, causing confusion and a slight delay at the LoDi orange line station."

"That's right," her co-anchor agreed, "and of course, let's not forget that just a few weeks ago, Grimsley made the shocking announcement that he was buying back a controlling stake in Grimsley Industries, which has been under the majority control of stockholders for almost thirty years. Grimsley used his own fortune to buy back the shares, and then he *donated* those shares to the School of Antiquity at the University of Templar, making the school dean Cheri Penderson arguably the most powerful woman in Pennsylvania."

"Possibly the entire mid-Atlantic," Lisa put in with a smile. "And in other news—"

Simon clicked off the TV and tossed the remote onto the table. "What do you make of that?" he asked.

"I have no idea," Virgil admitted. "I ride the subway all the time, and it's no big deal, but Peter Grimsley rides the subway, and it's our Top Story at Ten."

"No, not the subway part," Simon groaned, pinching the bridge of his nose. "The vanishing house."

"Oh," Virgil said. He blinked. "Yeah, that part's strange, too."

The front door opened, and a mail carrier walked in, his hat pulled down low on his head, his blue coat zipped all the way up to his throat against the autumn chill. He held up a thin stack of envelopes and tossed them onto Simon's table-desk. "Thanks," Simon murmured, still lost deeply in thought over the notion of a disappearing mansion.

The mailman gave him a lazy salute, then slipped back out the door.

Simon reached for the small stack of mail, but Virgil snatched the letters up first. "I love mail," he explained, flipping through the envelopes. "The problem with email is it doesn't get your hands dirty. I always say, if there's no chance of staining your fingers with ink or getting a papercut on your hand, is it really even worth reading?" He pulled out several marketing flyers and tossed them into the trash with a frown. "I could do without ads, though."

"Don't get *too* down on ads," Simon chimed in. "We're going to be in one soon."

"Yeah...but, like, a *digital* ad. I always say, if it's not digital, is it even worth reading?"

Simon rolled his eyes. Virgil was exhausting sometimes.

"Anything good?" he asked.

Virgil held up two envelopes. Both were larger than typical mailing envelopes. Both had been addressed to Dark Matter Investigations by hand. Neither had a return address.

Simon frowned. "Weird," he said. He chose the one on the left and plucked it out of Virgil's hand.

"Good choice," Virgil said. He turned over the manila envelope left in his own hands and tore it open. He pulled out a thin stack of papers, stapled together in the upper-left corner. He bit his bottom lip as he flipped through the pages.

"What is it?" Simon asked.

"I'm not sure..." He held the papers out.

Simon leaned forward to scrutinize them. The top page was a photocopy of some sort of ledger, or a roster. There was a table with thirty rows and three columns: the first column was titled *Name*; the second was *D.O.B.*; and the third was *Room*. The table was filled with names typed out in alphabetical order by last name, starting with Albert Axelrod and ending with Esther Derry.

"It's a list of old people," Simon said, confused. He pointed to the second column. "Look at the birthdays...the youngest one is..." He did some quick math. "Seventy-six? Seventy-seven?"

"Makes sense," Virgil decided, reading the roaster upside-down. "Look." He tapped his finger against the letterhead at the top of the page. The roster was printed beneath a logo for Caring Heart Nursing Home.

Simon flipped through the pages. There were seven of them in total, and each one was a similar roster, with names, dates of birth, and room numbers. Each was taken from a different nursing home or retirement community in Templar.

There was one other notable thing: each of the pages had red X's crossed through some of the room numbers.

"Are we supposed to know what this is about?" Virgil asked.

"I don't know. I mean, it must have something to do with Furtive Hills, right?"

Virgil looked down at the red X's. "You think the woman in the cloak kidnapped all these old people from their nursing homes?"

"I don't know if she *kidnapped* them. I think she lured them with the promise of restored youth."

Virgil frowned. He scratched his head absently, near the streak of hair that had turned gray. "So what's the point of the list? Why send it to us? We already stopped the Refracticore. There haven't been any more attacks."

"I don't know," Simon admitted. He sighed, rubbing his hands down his face. "It's just one piece of a big Shadow Lord puzzle."

"We really are pretty bad at being detectives," Virgil frowned. He picked up the open envelope and peered inside, checking to see if there was anything else. But it was empty. "No letter, no note—no nothing," he said. He turned it over, and his eyebrows arched with surprise. "Nothing except this."

He held out the envelope to Simon and tapped the bottom corner. The word "Templario" was written in capital letters.

"Templario?" Simon asked, confused. "What's a Templario?"

"Templario, my dear Simon, is the name of the Redditor who posted about Furtive Hills in the first place," Virgil said smugly. "I don't want to brag, but I think I found us our first real source."

"How does he have our address?" Simon asked.

"I sent it to him," Virgil replied.

"Great. Now we have to deal with a conspiracy theorist online *and* in real life," Simon groaned.

"We call that 'IRL,'" Virgil said helpfully. He snatched the papers away from Simon and waved them in the air. "And he's a conspiracy theorist who has access to private nursing home records! He's the real deal."

"He's probably a hacker, and now we're conspiring with a felon," Simon replied, turning in his chair. He glanced out the front window, and something strange caught his eye.

"You need to stop watching *Law and Order*," Virgil said, rolling his eyes. He stuffed the papers back into the manila envelope and tossed it onto the desk. "You going to open yours?" he asked.

"Yeah, sorry," Simon replied. "I was just..." He stood up from his chair and craned his neck, trying to get a better view of the street. "Did you see that?" he asked, pointing toward the sidewalk.

"See what?" Virgil followed his friend's gaze, but didn't see anything unusual.

Simon frowned. "Nothing, I guess. I thought..." He rubbed his eyes and shook his head. "Never mind. I thought I saw the mailman throw the mailbag into the dumpster."

"Why would a mailman throw his mailbag into a dumpster?" Virgil asked.

"I don't know," Simon said, stepping out from behind the table and crossing over to the windows. "I don't think I'm seeing straight. I didn't sleep too well last night. I had the weirdest dream..."

He moved to the window and watched as the mailman stepped quickly down the stairs that led to the subway. From the distance and the angle, he couldn't tell if the man still had his bag on his shoulder or not.

"Sorry," he apologized to Virgil over his shoulder. "I think my eyes are playing tricks on me."

"It's your old age," Virgil replied, picking up the second piece of mail. "You're a full year older than me, so it makes sense you'd start losing your vision first." He turned the envelope over and slid his thumb beneath the flap.

Simon furrowed his brow, his mind clicking as the gears in his brain began to turn. "Why would a mailman use the subway instead of a delivery truck?" he said quietly, more to himself than to Virgil. "Why would a mailman...?"

Then the gears clicked into place.

A mailman *wouldn't* use the subway instead of a delivery truck.

That's something an imposter would do.

"Virgil!" he cried. "Stop!"

But he was too late. Virgil had already torn open the envelope.

CHAPTER 9

Darkness erupted from the envelope like a bomb in Virgil's hand—an actual, *tangible* darkness, thick and black and dense, like an explosion of tar.

Virgil dove backward, scrambling to the far end of the office. The thick, gooey, black mass expanded to the size of a trampoline, then dropped to the floor, fast and hard. And then it went *beyond* the floor, pulling downward in the middle, like a funnel. Simon's table, which sat just a few feet from the black mass, began to rattle, as if it were feeling the tremors of an earthquake. The chair shook, too, and Simon and Virgil watched with horror as the chair began to slide toward the hole in the floor, slow and halting at first, skidding a few inches, stopping, skidding a few more inches, stopping again...and then the black funnel began to spin, its edges swirling unevenly around the hole like soap suds spinning around a drain, and the chair picked up speed, sliding all the way over to the hole and tipping down into it.

The table went next, crashing end-over-end, falling into the funnel and disappearing into the inky blackness.

"*Shadow pit!*" Virgil screamed.

Simon didn't know what a shadow pit was, except to say he knew unequivocally that it described exactly the thing in the center of the office. In the same way that Virgil had put the perfect title to the Shadow Lord, he had managed to give the right name to the swirling black hole, too.

"Move!" Simon cried. He dove toward the door and had gotten a hand on the glass when he was struck with a realization that made his heart sink.

The office didn't have an exit out the back. The only other door to the outside was on the side of the building.

Simon was half a step away from safety, but Virgil was trapped.

"Simon!" Virgil cried, his voice tight. "Help!"

The shadow pit was slowly growing larger, its spinning edges spreading further and further across the floor. The television rattled on its shelf, barely able to resist the high-gravity pull of the deep, dark mass on the floor. The moldering recliner creaked and groaned as it went skidding across the linoleum, then went tumbling down into the pit, where the hungry, churning shadows swallowed it up like quicksand.

Simon even felt the hairs on his arms shift toward the hole.

He looked down at his jacket. The hem had lifted into the air, as if being pulled by an invisible string. "Oh, no," he whispered.

He looked across the room and saw Virgil lurch forward. "Simon!" he screamed, his face white with terror. The gravity of the shadow pit was drawing him closer to the edge. Virgil struggled backward, fighting against the pull, but his back was against the wall. He started edging closer to the door that led to the back room, but Simon knew that wouldn't save him; it would only buy him time. Without an exit, the pit would claim him eventually.

In the end, it didn't even matter. Virgil took one more step toward the door, but his foot slipped, yanked sideways by the gravity of the pit, and he hit the ground, hard, and began to slide across the floor toward the shadows.

"*Simon!*"

Simon broke from his trance. He sprinted forward, running toward the spinning pit. The gravity tugged him forward, and he moved like a shot across the room. He charged up his hands as he dove forward, over the lip of the swirling, black shadow mass. He formed a powerful shield in his left hand and held the energy in his right hand in the center of his fist. As the shadow pit sucked him into its dark funnel, he threw the shield downward from its broad, flat surface. It stuck in the bottom of the pit like a penny wedged flatwise in a funnel, and he crashed down onto it, using it like a platform. He bounced once and jumped up across the open pit, firing the blast from his right hand down onto the shield as he rose up into the air. The force of the magical blast propelled him upward like a rocket, shooting him up and out of the pit, onto the far side of the shadow trap.

He landed hard, and a shock of pain shot through his ankle as he hit the linoleum floor. He sucked in air through his teeth, biting back the pain as he reached down and helped Virgil to his feet. The shield had dampened the gravitational pull a bit, but he didn't know how long the kinesthetic energy would last. "Let's move!" he said.

Virgil jumped down into the pit first, and Simon leapt in half a beat after. Virgil hit the shield and jumped back up, firing thrusts out of both of his hands. He sailed up into the air as Simon hit the shield right behind him. Simon moved to jump up, too, but the surface of the shield cracked under his weight, and it broke in half just as he was pushing off. He stumbled as he jumped, and even with the propulsion bursts from both of his hands, he wasn't able to clear the top of the funnel. With the shield barrier broken, the shadow trap's gravity was back in full effect, and it pulled Simon down toward its all-consuming darkness.

Virgil hit the ground outside of the spinning circle, nearly falling backward into it, wind-milling his arms to keep himself on his feet. He turned when he heard the shield crack, and he watched as Simon fell backward toward the bottom of the funnel.

"Simon!" he screamed.

Simon fired up his left hand and threw his arm up toward the ceiling. Acting on total instinct, he focused the energy blast into a long, thin rope. It extended from his palm, waving and unfurling like a whip as it stretched through the air. The far end of the glowing orange rope sped up toward Virgil. Virgil reached out to grab the end of the whip, and the whip grabbed him instead, twining around his wrist and locking into place. Simon grabbed ahold of the other end, twisting the glowing rope around his hand to get a better grip, and he held on tight. "Pull!" he yelled.

Virgil gripped the rope with both hands and tried hauling it backward over the lip of the shadow funnel. But the gravity of the trap was powerful, and even with Virgil using all his strength, the suction force pulled him, his sneakers screeching against the linoleum as they were dragged forward. Virgil let go of the rope with his right hand. He powered up his fist and slammed it into the floor with a warrior's cry. His fist blasted deep into the floor, crashing through the linoleum and the concrete, digging down past his wrist. Anchored by his hand, he held himself in place, the veins of his neck popping out against his skin from the strain of being pulled down toward the black hole.

"Simon!" he grunted through clenched teeth. "I—can't hold it!"

Simon held tightly to his end of the glowing rope, pressing against the swirling, sloping side of the shadow trap funnel. The shadows that rushed past him were cold, and they felt wet, as if he were lying on his side in a shallow but powerful creek. The bottom of the funnel sucked at his shoes; it took every ounce of strength he could muster to pull his knees up to keep from having his feet get sucked down into the shadow trap. He reached down with one trembling hand and cast another shield, but from his awkward position, the angle was wrong, and he couldn't throw it perfectly flat on top of the funnel hole. The shield skidded down on its edge instead, then got caught in the swirling eddy of shadows and disappeared down into the inky blackness, falling through the shadow trap.

He heard Virgil crying out, begging him to hurry. He reached back up with his free hand and tried to grab the rope to pull himself out, but he didn't have the strength, and the pull of the shadow was too powerful. His hand slid back down the rope, and he was left to twist in the cold, wet rush of shadows spinning past him.

Just when he had given up hope, a memory flashed through his head: he saw himself at the edge of the clearing on the Stocks, furious and tired. He saw his hands pushing into the soft dirt, and he watched as small flowers grew and bloomed around him, releasing their tiny, glowing ball bearings, the ones that rose into the air, hovered for a breath, then pinged through the clearing like the spread from a circle of shotguns.

A calm washed over Simon, and he closed his eyes. He reached up with his free hand, palm open to the ceiling. He envisioned those glowing orange balls of light now, and they formed above his hand...first just one, then another, then another, until there were dozens of tiny, magical orbs floating in the midst of the swirling shadow. He pushed them upward with an invisible force, and they filled the funnel like fireflies.

Then Simon flicked his wrist, and each ball burst into a long thread, stretching from one end of the funnel to the other, each one giving off a soft *twang* like guitar strings.

All through the air above him, the threads shot across the funnel, forming a three-dimensional web that led to the top of the trap. The ends of the threads swirled downward with the suction of the shadows, slowly sinking toward the bottom. Simon had to act fast. He reached up and grabbed the nearest thread, and it held. He let go of the orange rope and grabbed the next thread up. That one held, too, and as the Cat's Cradle web of orange wires circled the funnel, Simon circled with them, pulling himself up the strings, finding purchase with his feet and climbing the web like scaffolding.

The pull of the shadow was strong, but Simon's threads were stronger. It took all of his strength, but he managed to creep up through the rotating scaffold, up to the top of the shadow trap. Virgil, having released his end of the rope, let go of the hole in the concrete floor and slid carefully forward, grabbing Simon's hands and pulling him up through the web and onto the safety of the linoleum.

Breathing hard, lying on his side, Simon turned back toward the shadow trap and extended his hand toward the threads. He closed his hand into a fist, and the threads pulled tight…and when they did, they cinched the shadow trap shut, pulling the floor together like a bag being closed tight by a drawstring.

The pull of gravity stopped.

The shadow trap was gone.

CHAPTER 10

"Next time we make an enemy, can it please be someone who doesn't work so hard to try to make us dead?" Virgil grumped.

They both lay on the linoleum floor, out of breath and exhausted. "It could be worse," Simon wheezed. "We could have actually died."

"I'd prefer a scenario where we're not so surprised and delighted to still be alive."

Simon propped himself up on his elbows and looked out over the office. The place where his magical threads had cinched the floor together was seamless, as if the shadow trap had never happened.

Virgil struggled up to a seat, too, his face marked by a troubled thought. "How did you do that thing with all the threads?" he asked gently, his voice a mixture of awe and caution. "And the whip, too. How did you know how to do those things? We didn't learn anything like that from Llewyn."

Simon hesitated. He continued to look down at the floor, avoiding eye contact with his friend. He had meant to bring up the new ways his powers had been manifesting—how he had made the ball-bearing plants in the Stocks, and how he had shot two streams of constant flame-thrower magic from his hands. He had meant to talk with Virgil about this, and about how the magic just seemed to *happen* in those moments, like his brain switched off and the power took over. But he didn't know how to bring it up without sounding boastful, or how to express the idea that the magic acting on its own like that scared him, the way it took control. So he had kept putting it off, and putting it off.

But he couldn't put it off any longer.

"I don't know," he said truthfully, still looking down at the floor. The tips of his ears burned with heat. "It just...*happens*." He talked about the magic he'd created while Virgil had been under attack by the Refracticore's energy column.

Virgil listened with his mouth hanging open. "That...is *awesome!*" he said when Simon had finished.

"Yeah?" Simon asked cautiously, raising an eyebrow.

"Simon! Yes!" Virgil jumped excitedly to his feet. "It's so cool! Your power is...I don't know! Growing! It's...*evolving!*" He looked down at his own hands with wonder. "*I* want evolving powers," he decided. He tried making something incredible happen with his magic. His palms shot a few sparks that fizzled out in the air. Virgil frowned. "Maybe after I eat lunch," he decided.

"Come on, Virg—are you kidding me?" Simon asked. He nodded to the hole in the floor just a few feet away. "You literally *punched through concrete* with your *bare hand!* That's pretty evolved."

Virgil grinned. "Yeah...that *was* pretty cool," he admitted, flexing the fingers of his right hand. "I'm like Iron Fist. The *comic book* version of Iron First, *not* the Netflix version," he added quickly. "But it wasn't a finesse move. Your moves are *finesse* moves." The smile faded from his face, and he considered Simon thoughtfully. "I think you've got more sorcery in you than anyone realizes," he said.

Simon opened his mouth to respond to that, but just then, the strangest sound filled the room. It was the sound of an extraordinarily loud zipper being pulled, and it echoed so loudly that Simon had to clap his hands over his ears to keep his head from rattling.

The sound came from the back of the office, and when they turned to look, they saw the entire back wall peel away from one corner like a piece of thin fabric. A seam had opened up along the side of the wall where it connected with the main exterior wall, and the opening grew longer and longer, until it reached the top of the building. Then it did a ninety-degree turn and began to run along the length of the ceiling, as if someone were actually unzipping the wall.

They watched with amazement as the solid structure became as thin and wavering as a sheet, collapsing as the seam unzipped along the entire ceiling. When it hit the other corner, the seam headed back down to the floor, until the entire wall was unzipped. It fluttered to the floor.

Morgaine peered into the office from behind the new opening, smirking with disapproval.

"*This* is where you conduct your affairs?"

Simon gaped at the sight that now filled his vision. On the other side of the fallen office wall, Morgaine stood on a ruined flagstone floor, with cracked and battered stone-and-timber walls rising up behind her.

He was staring out of his office and into Llewyn's mansion, as if the wizard's tent were a built-on addition to the old laundromat building.

"Did you...*move* our building?" Virgil asked, incredulous. He looked over his shoulder to make sure they were still in the old strip mall.

Morgaine stepped through the opening, frowning down at the stained linoleum floor. "Of course not. Moving a building is cumbersome. It leads to all sorts of questions." Simon and Virgil both flashed back to the news report on Grimsley Manor. "I didn't move your building; I simply stitched it to Llewyn's."

"Why?" Simon asked, watching Morgaine as she walked slowly through the old laundromat, looking over every inch with disgust.

"I was curious to see where you do your...*work*," she said, pronouncing the word *work* as if it tasted horrible on her tongue. "I thought that perhaps three young people who have the power and the fortitude to both summon and release Morgan le Fay might be three young people worth keeping an eye on. I can't leave Llewyn for long, he's in a rather fragile state—he's *fine*," she added quickly, holding up her hand to stop them from asking as soon as she saw them open their mouths. "He is in several fewer pieces than he was when you saw him last. He's mending. But it is a delicate process, and I must remain close. Still...I was curious about your seat of power." She wrinkled up her nose in disappointment. "This is...not what I expected."

"We just moved in," Simon explained, blushing a little. "It's not done yet."

Morgaine snorted. "I should say not." She did a full spin, taking in the entire, empty room. "Where do you...*do* things? There's not even a place to sit."

"Well, we had a recliner," Virgil informed her. "But it just got swallowed up by the floor." He scratched the back of the neck. "Along with the table. And the folding chair."

Morgaine arched an eyebrow, looking at Virgil with interest. "Swallowed up by the floor?" she said.

Simon shifted uncomfortably. "We had a—well, it's—um...we have this...problem—"

"It's like a nemesis," Virgil said. "We have a nemesis. The Shadow Lord."

"Yeah," Simon said. "He just sent us a shadow trap. Like a black hole shadow vortex thing."

"It ate all our furniture," Virgil said.

Morgaine nodded sagely. "I see. I assume this trap was delivered by some sort of steward of this Shadow Lord?"

"He was dressed like a mailman," Virgil nodded.

"Mm. And have you wreaked your terrible vengeance on this creature?" she asked.

Simon started. "Have we...wreaked our terrible vengeance on him?" he said, confused.

"Yes, yes," Morgaine replied, twirling her hand in the air, as if trying to hurry along this obvious part of the conversation. "Did you capture him and make him suffer for playing a sinister role in your would-be demise?"

"We don't make people suffer!" Simon said, shocked. "And we don't 'wreak vengeance.'"

"We're the good guys," Virgil added helpfully.

Morgaine scoffed. "Anyone who holds to that simply hasn't been pushed far enough yet," she sneered.

"And secondly," Simon continued, choosing to ignore that comment, "we couldn't have done anything to him if we wanted; we were a little busy fighting the black hole that opened up in the middle of our office and tried to swallow us whole."

"I punched through concrete," Virgil said proudly.

"And you haven't replayed time?" Morgaine asked.

Simon blinked. Virgil cocked his head to the side. "What?" they both said in unison.

Morgaine rolled her eyes and sighed, as if dealing with these two magical novices was the single-most trying experience of her life. "You are students of Llewyn Dughlasach of Moray of the Highlands, your magic is dynagogical, is it not?"

"Yeah..." Virgil said slowly.

"And did your frozen friend explain to you that dynagogical magic works on the principle of kinetic-mystical ley lines, which emanate from a time-resistant plane?"

"Something like that," Simon said uncertainly. He remembered Llewyn mentioning the fact that time worked differently on the dynagogical plane, but he couldn't remember if he'd learned much more than that...

"The magic that you tap into is uniquely suited to time manipulation."

"Wait, wait, wait," Virgil said, waving his hands through the air, "are you saying that we can *time travel?*"

Morgaine smirked. "I am saying that small bursts of time manipulation are not beyond the purview of your powers."

Virgil gaped at her. He turned to Simon. "Llewyn sort of forgot to mention that part," he said.

"It's not surprising," Morgaine continued, walking slowly around the room with her hands clasped behind her back, now suddenly a patient and knowledgeable professor, with her long, blue dress trailing behind her on the floor. "Llewyn has ever been an overly-cautious sort. He'd be more concerned with the potential pitfalls of time manipulation than with the extraordinary benefits."

Simon knew he should be wary when it came to the suggestions of Morgan le Fay, but he had grown up on *Back to the Future* and *Donnie Darko,* and he couldn't help it; the idea of time travel piqued his interest. "What sort of pitfalls?" he asked cautiously.

"Oh, multiple timelines, temporal distortions, time loops, alternate futures," she said dismissively. "If you ask me, it's all nonsense, really. People always assume that unnaturally-manipulated time redirections are mutations of a pre-determined timeline, but they never stop to consider that perhaps those tweaks were *part* of the pre-destined timeline all along."

The conversation was suddenly getting a little heady for Virgil. "So you're saying we could go back in time and stop the delivery guy from bringing us the shadow trap?"

"I'm saying it's your right as dynagogical wizards to play that particular card, if you'd like," she said, clearly pleased with herself.

"But we'd be creating a different version of the future," Simon pointed out. "A different version of now. I think maybe Llewyn's right to be wary of that sort of thing." He turned to Morgaine. "You think it's weakness, but Llewyn cares about the impact of his magic on other people."

Morgaine snorted and sauntered off across the room. "Your choice," she called over her shoulder.

"We don't have to change the timeline," Virgil said, sounding more and more excited as the idea unfurled in his mind. "We could go back, and let the guy deliver the shadow trap, but this time we can follow him down to the subway and see where he goes. He might even lead us straight to the lair of the Shadow Lord!"

"You think the Shadow Lord lives off the orange line?" Simon asked doubtfully.

"I think we should find out," Virgil replied, his eyes bright with excitement.

"It's easily enough done," Morgaine offered from across the room, though she sounded a little disappointed by the somewhat less-intrusive use of time manipulation that Virgil was proposing.

Simon considered the plan. If they let everything play out exactly as it had the first time, what harm could there be, really? If they could do it without interfering in the events of the original timeline, and if they just followed the deliveryman to see where he went, without engaging him, it would really just be research, and potentially invaluable research at that. "We *just* follow, and we don't engage," Simon clarified.

"Works for me," Virgil shrugged. He grinned broadly and said, "Let's do it, Simon. Holy Hamburg. Let's be *time travelers*!"

CHAPTER 11

"One thing first," Morgaine said, and the smile evaporated from Virgil's face.

"I knew there'd be a catch," he grumbled.

Morgaine stepped into the center of the room. "It's not a catch; it's just this...*place*," she said disgustedly, putting out her hands as if she were trying to hold back the awfulness of the old laundromat. Her mouth turned downward into a sour frown. "I can't possibly concentrate on time manipulation when I'm standing on dirty linoleum beneath fluorescent lighting."

"It was the only building in our budget," Simon said quietly.

"The bounce house was in our budget," Virgil reminded him bitterly.

Morgaine ignored them both. "I trust you won't mind if I make a few improvements?"

"What sort of improvements?" Simon asked.

But Morgaine wasn't listening. She closed her eyes and lifted her arms above her head, crossing them at the wrist. Her lips moved as she recited a silent spell, and as she worked, her entire body began to give off a gentle blue glow. Tiny sparks of light materialized at the edges of the room and zoomed toward her, streaking through the air like shooting stars. They gathered around her hands, creating a swirling orb of gentle light. Then she threw her hands down, and the orb smashed against the floor, exploding in a bright ball of fire that burst across the room, filling it with smoke and heat and light.

Simon and Virgil screamed. They fell to the ground, waving their arms like mad, warding off the flames...but the instant after the fire had filled the room, it had dissipated, leaving behind just a thick curtain of smoke. They hacked and coughed, clearing out their lungs, waving the dark gray smoke away from their stinging, watery eyes.

When the smoke cleared, they gasped in amazement.

The room was completely changed.

Gone was the linoleum floor, the peeling vinyl replaced by deep, rich wooden planks that were covered by a series of beautiful, carefully-woven rugs. The fluorescent lights that had hung from the ceiling were gone, replaced by three chandeliers, two smaller brass fixtures flanking a large, ornate central chandelier with crystals dripping down from the sconces. The dirty, off-white walls were now covered in a dark-blue wallpaper with elegant light-gray floral patterns, and there was framed art on the walls, stately paintings of Victorian men and women performing various magic spells. One painting featured a short, fat gentleman with a top hat, a monocle, and a walrus mustache, clutching an umbrella in one hand and shooting red flames out of the other, aiming them at some unseen foe just off to the side of the canvas. Another painting showed a straight-backed woman in a high-throated dress with a full bustle and a wide-brimmed hat levitating above a trio of fearful-looking men, surrounded by an outwardly expanding series of green auras.

A fireplace had inserted itself into the wall beneath the painting of the woman, an impressive, stone-laid hearth that was wider than Simon would be if he stretched both of his arms out to either side. Logs crackled in the fireplace, their flames bathing the white stone in a warm and rosy light.

The office now had two identical desks, both made of hand-carved mahogany. They were stately pieces, with a dark stain and drawers that opened by way of silver-flourish knobs. The desks had matching armchairs as well, dark green leather on locked wheels.

A third desk had been placed in the far corner of the room, along with a modest couch and a brown-leather chaise lounge. It was a semi-private corner now, cordoned off from the rest of the office by a six-panel accordion divider that boasted hand-painted gold flourishes against a dark blue background that was the same color as the walls.

An old fashioned wooden file cabinet stood against one wall. The television and its precariously-balanced platform had disappeared altogether, and in their place, a large LCD flat-screen had been mounted on the side wall.

There was a new waiting area, too, at the front of the building, with two comfortable-looking benches lining the wall on either side of the door, upholstered in the same green leather as the desk chairs. A low wooden wall topped with frosted panes of glass separated the waiting area from the rest of the space.

"There," Morgaine said, glancing around and smiling with pleasure. "*Now* it's a proper office."

Simon and Virgil padded slowly around the room, marveling at the splendor of the space. "It's incredible," Simon murmured with awe.

Virgil plopped down in one of the desk chairs and spun around in a circle, coming to a stop with his feet propped up on the desk. "All it's missing is a bounce house," he said with a smile.

"I suppose if we're updating things, I shouldn't exempt myself," Morgaine said, looking down at her dress. "I don't guess 'royal wench' is still in vogue." She made a large flourish with one hand, and her dress faded away in a downward spiral, starting at her shoulders and spinning down to the hem below her ankles. As it disappeared, it was seamlessly replaced by new fabrics, and when the effect was complete, Morgaine was wearing a loose, long-sleeve, blue cotton t-shirt over a pair of knit yoga pants with black-and-gray sharkskin stitching. A pair of white sneakers completed the outfit. She glanced down, twisting to the side and admiring her new look. "The future is comfort," she said approvingly. Then she looked up at Simon and Virgil, and her smile faded. "What you're wearing is...fine," she decided.

She shook back her sleeves so they fell to her elbows, and she rubbed her hands together excitedly. Her lips curled up into a dangerous grin. "Now," she said, with a lock of her dark, wild hair slashing across her brow. "Shall we begin?"

She pressed her palms together and held them out in front of her, parallel with the floor. An aqua-blue light shined through the spaces between her fingers, and she pulled her hands apart, revealing a small blue bead encased in circular metal bands. The sphere spun lazily in the air, and through the rotating metal bands, they could see a purple smoke trail swirling around within the blue light of the orb.

"What is that?" Simon breathed, mesmerized by the beauty of the thing.

"It's a time capsule," Morgaine said, her eyes large and filled with something like desire as she stared down into the swirling mists.

"We can make those?" Virgil asked, his voice quiet with awe.

"After you receive the proper training, yes." Morgaine reached up and touched the time capsule with two fingers, and the metal bands immediately responded to her touch. They stacked themselves one on top of the other, with a quick *clack-clack-clack* sound. The bottom half of the ball she held between her fingers was now gray metal, and the top half was the shimmering blue light.

She reached down with her free hand and placed the tips of her fingers on the blue surface. The clouds of purple within the orb gathered at the points where her skin made contact with the capsule. "Ready?" she asked, glancing over at Simon and Virgil.

Virgil had pushed himself up from the desk chair, and now the two of them were standing shoulder-to-shoulder, inching toward the time capsule, hypnotized by its beauty. "Ready," they said in unison.

Morgaine looked back at the time capsule and said, "They're with me." Then she gave the top half of the capsule a hard counter-clockwise twist, and time slammed into them like a tidal wave.

CHAPTER 12

Virgil opened his eyes. He stumbled to the right and almost fell.

Time travel made him dizzy.

"Did we do it?" he asked. But he didn't need to wait for an answer. A quick glance around was enough for him to know that they had gone back.

The office was once again an abandoned laundromat, with its rust-stained floor and glaring fluorescent lights. The back room was still a back room, perfectly attached to the rest of the building, and the recliner, the table-desk, and the folding chair were in their proper places.

"This is wild," Virgil decided.

Simon looked around the room, trying to settle his dizzy head and hoping he wouldn't throw up on the floor. "When are we?" he asked.

"This morning," Morgaine confirmed. "The two of you and your purple-haired friend are on your way here. I thought I'd set us down before you arrived, so as to avoid any complicated confrontations with yourselves."

"Wait, so we're here, *and* we're there? At the same time?"

"Yes, of course," Morgaine said. "And I suggest you remove yourselves from the building before you arrive. Side effects of meeting one's future self have been known to include heart burstings and brain aneurysms."

"Aren't you coming with us?" Simon asked, suddenly alarmed. He didn't trust Morgaine one bit, and having her near gave him a prickling sense of doom that he couldn't quite shake...but she was also their time-travel guide, the touchstone to their future-present, and walking around in the past without her would be like walking around on Mars without a tether. "You have to come with us, right?"

"I think I'll stay and see this shadow trap," she said. "Get a sense for how your Shadow Lord works."

"Why?" Simon asked suspiciously.

Morgaine smirked. "Because I'm new in town, and I want to get a lay of the social order."

"You can't just let us go wandering out there by ourselves," Virgil said. "We will almost *definitely* break the past."

"You can't break the past. You can only restyle it."

"How will we get back to the present?" Simon demanded.

"You won't," Morgaine shrugged. "You'll overlap your present time in less than an hour. Once that happens, the present will be replaced with the *new* present. As long as you don't change anything, everything should carry on as it otherwise would have."

"And if we do change something?" Virgil asked.

"Then it won't matter, because every moment after your present is currently unwritten. Whatever you do will *determine* the present. You will be about an hour older than you were when you traveled backward, though. You'll want to check with Llewyn for a life-extending spell to make up for that at some point. If he wakes up."

"*If* he wakes up?!" Simon cried.

"*When*—I meant *when* he wakes up. Now go," she said, shooing them with her hands. They felt a strong, invisible force push at them from behind, scooting them toward the door. "You'll be here in a moment, and you don't want you to see you."

Simon opened his mouth to protest, but before he could utter a word, they were pushed out the front door and deposited into the parking lot.

They stood on the asphalt and looked at each other, bewildered.

"I think we made a big mistake," Simon said.

"With the time travel?" Virgil asked.

Simon turned back to the office and looked at Morgaine through the windows. She headed toward the back of the office, slowly turning herself invisible as she went. "With all of it," Simon sighed.

Then they jogged across the street and ducked behind a parked van just as Simon's Pontiac 6000LE pulled around the corner.

CHAPTER 13

"You said my gray streak looked distinguished," Virgil said, watching his past self enter the Dark Matter office from across the street.

"Actually, *you* said it looks distinguished," Simon pointed out. "I just didn't disagree with you out loud."

Virgil frowned. "I look like a *Beetlejuice* character," he said.

It was strange watching themselves get out of the car and head into the building. Abby pulled up after them in her truck, and Simon felt a little guilty as he watched her hop down from the driver's seat and cross the parking lot. "I feel like a stalker," he muttered.

"Better to be a stalker than some Tim Burton Netherworld monster," Virgil grumped.

They watched the office until Larry the herpetomorph showed up and went inside. They knew Abby would be busy with her session for the next half hour, and that Simon and Virgil would be getting into an argument about the Dark Matter Investigations sign soon, and no one would be looking out the windows, so they chanced a move and ran into the Church's Chicken to grab a couple of sodas while they waited for the steward of the Shadow Lord.

"You know, the sign actually looks pretty good from here," Virgil admitted, staring out across the street.

"You don't have to say that," Simon said.

"I don't know, maybe it's the different perspective," Virgil shrugged. "Or maybe it's the fact that I know the whole awful *inside* of the place is going to get sucked down a black hole and be replaced by a whole Sherlock Holmes aesthetic that has me feeling better about the *outside*." He sucked down his orange Slice and shook the ice in the cup. "Either way. The sign looks pretty good."

"Thanks."

They chatted a bit over refills, glancing nervously out the window every few seconds, waiting for the fake postal worker. Finally, he appeared, emerging from the subway stairs in his dark blue uniform and heading straight toward Dark Matter Investigations.

"Here we go," Simon said, finishing off his drink and tossing it into the trash on the way to the door. "Remember: we're not interfering. We're just following."

"No interfering," Virgil confirmed.

"Because sometimes you like to interfere in things, and I just want to be clear—"

"Simon!" Virgil said, sounding hurt. "I know how to be subtle, okay?"

"You once wrapped yourself in battery-powered Christmas lights from head to toe," Simon reminded him.

"I was sharing the holiday spirit!" Virgil cried.

"It was April!"

"And people were grateful for a little holiday cheer!"

"Look," Simon said, pinching the bridge of his nose, "I'm just saying: our goal is to blend in, to not interfere, and to *not* change the timeline."

"Well, let's hurry up and blend in fast, because we're about to lose him again." Virgil nodded out the Church's Chicken door, and Simon turned just in time to see the mailman toss his bag down the alley two buildings over from them and disappear down the subway stairs.

"Come on," Simon said.

They hurried over to the top of the stairs, sparing a quick glance at their offices, where inside, they knew, the shadow trap had just exploded full-force and was busy sucking the furniture down its gullet.

"Stay strong," Virgil said, sending his past self some good vibes.

Then they headed down the stairs, following the shadow-servant underground.

CHAPTER 14

"Does it always smell like this?" Simon asked, wrinkling his nose at the stench in the air.

"Not always," Virgil said, swiping his card and pushing through the turnstile. "Sometimes, it's worse."

Simon wasn't much for public transportation. It wasn't that he didn't appreciate the idea of mass transit, but the Templar subway system seemed to go pretty much everywhere *except* the places he wanted to go. There were no stops near their apartment, or by Squeezy Cheez, or by Llewyn's drainage ditch, and honestly, those were basically the only places he went anymore, aside from the new Dark Matter office. "It's awful down here," he observed.

There was another set of concrete stairs that led down to the train platform, and they peeked down to make sure the shadow-servant wasn't lurking in the stairwell. The walls of the subway station were covered in grime, and the floor was inexplicably wet. The steps themselves were crumbling in several spots, and Simon had to be mindful of where he stepped, or else he'd twist an ankle.

"Yeah, the orange line isn't great," Virgil agreed. "I mean, none of the lines are going to win Best in Show, but the orange line is especially bad."

Unlike Simon, Virgil actually liked to ride the subway from time to time, even though it didn't really take him anywhere he wanted to go, either. Sometimes he would just hop on a train and ride it around beneath the city, jumping off at random stops and heading up above ground to explore a part of town he'd never seen before. He'd tried to get Simon to tag along a few times, insisting that it was important to ride the subway so that they didn't lose touch with the city. But Simon could never shake a certain feeling of dread when he thought about riding in a cramped, closed train car beneath a few solid tons of earth and concrete, and so he stuck to the Pontiac whenever he could.

Which was basically always.

"I think I finally understand why everyone freaked out when Peter Grimsley took the subway," Simon grimaced, pulling his hand away from a mysteriously sticky spot on the handrail.

"Don't be elitist," Virgil chided. They crouched when they were about halfway down the second set of stairs, peering down at the platform below and scanning it for the shadow-servant. "There," Virgil said, pointing down at the far end. "Looks like he's going west."

The imposter mailman was standing near the edge of the platform. As they watched, he plucked the U. S. Post Office-issued hat off his head and tossed it into a nearby trashcan. Then he unzipped his coat, shrugged out of it, and tossed that into the trashcan, too. The man was tall, and older than them, maybe in his thirties, with wavy brown hair. "Any chance he looks familiar to you?" Simon asked.

"Nope," Virgil replied.

Simon couldn't help but wonder how vast the Shadow Lord's army might be, and how many of the strangers they passed every day might count themselves among his servants.

The idea of the army's potential limitlessness sent shivers down his spine.

Suddenly, there was the loud squeal of metal rubbing against metal, and the train screeched into the station. Simon and Virgil crept down the stairs, careful to stay out of the man's peripheral vision. The doors to the train cars opened, and a handful of people stepped off the subway and onto the platform. Dodging through the small crowd, Simon and Virgil stepped quickly but carefully forward, watching the shadow-servant enter the very first car. Simon and Virgil hurried closer to the front end of the train, and they ducked inside the back of the second car just as the warning sound chimed and the doors slid shut.

They could see the shadow-servant in the next car through the windows.

"I don't think he saw us," Simon said, relaxing a little. The man had sat down in a seat with his back to their car, so they could see him, but he couldn't see them without turning around.

They eased themselves forward through the car as it rumbled along, and they grabbed a pair of seats near the front, making sure there was plenty of room to duck out of the way if the shadow-servant did turn in their direction.

"What do we do now?" Virgil asked.

"I guess we see where he gets off, and we follow him. See if he takes us to the Shadow Lord."

Virgil furrowed his brow. He tapped his bottom lip with his teeth, lost in thought for a few moments. "What do we do if, like…he *does* take us to the Shadow Lord?" he asked, his voice lined with an edge of nervousness.

Simon frowned. He hadn't really considered their next steps. "I guess we decide whether or not to confront him."

Virgil nodded miserably. "We really should have brought Morgaine," he said.

The train rumbled on through several more stops, traveling west for several miles before turning and bending north, toward the Juniata River. Each time the train left a station, it plunged into another concrete tunnel, and the only lights in that space beneath the earth were the ones provided by the train itself. Otherwise, the tunnels were dark, and cold, and grimy, and wet, and so small and suffocating that Simon could have opened a window and placed his entire palm against the curving concrete surface.

"I don't like it down here," he whispered, watching the grease- and rust-streaked cement flash past the glass.

"It's bigger than your car," Virgil said, trying to soothe his friend. "You could fit two Pontiacs in this train car."

Simon nodded absently. "Yeah," he said. "But if I have to, I can get out of my car and run."

He felt trapped, and it was suddenly hard to breathe.

Simon closed his eyes and placed a hand against his chest, trying to convince his heart to slow its rapid beating. Beads of sweat were collecting on his forehead, and he squirmed as he felt a drop trickle down his spine, between his shoulder blades. He forced himself to take a slow, deep breath, and then to exhale it just as slowly. But when he did, he felt like he was suffocating, like he wasn't forcing enough air into his lungs. So he breathed faster again, quick, shallow breaths that left him light-headed.

"Hey...Simon...are you okay?" Virgil asked. His voice sounded like it was reaching Simon from the bottom of a well.

"I don't like close spaces," he whispered. His throat was dry, and the words came out in a hard rasp.

"Okay. Okay," Virgil said, trying to sound calm, despite the fact that his friend was on the verge of a full-blown panic attack. He nodded out the window. "Look, it's opening up. There's more space."

And indeed, the close tunnel fell away as they passed into a larger chamber beneath the ground. It was like making it to the inside of an igloo after passing through the narrow, icy entrance. They were still underground, they were still closed in, and Simon still felt trapped, but at least now he knew that he could step off the train if he had to, if there was an emergency, and walk around a little. It wasn't great in this bigger part of the tunnel, but it was better.

His breath came more easily as the train screeched along the tracks, and his heartbeat began to slow.

He looked up at the car in front of them, and the man with the wavy brown hair was turned around in his seat, staring into their car, locking eyes with Simon.

The shadow-servant jumped to his feet.

Then the subway lost power, and all the lights blinked off, plunging the entire train into complete and total darkness.

CHAPTER 15

It took Simon almost ten full seconds to realize that the screams he was hearing were coming from his own throat.

"Simon!" Virgil said, giving his friend a hard shake.

Simon came back to himself, and he stopped shouting. He sat there, gasping in the darkness, trying desperately to fill his lungs. "Virgil!" he cried, reaching out and digging his fingers into Virgil's arm. "What's happening?"

"Simon. Calm down." Virgil pulled out his phone and tapped the flashlight on. The bright light gave their end of the train car an otherworldly glow. The seats threw long, misshapen shadows against the metal walls. "You're having a panic attack. But we're okay. The train just lost power. It happens. It's an old subway. It'll be back on in a minute."

"I can't breathe," Simon said, tugging at his collar, trying to open his airway. "Virgil, I can't breathe!"

"I know, but listen," Virgil said quietly, leaning in closer, "I think you're freaking out the other people on the train."

"The other—?" Simon had somehow forgotten that there were other people in their car. He craned his neck and looked over his shoulder. There were four other riders, all sitting toward the back of the car, pointing their phone flashlights in his direction. Their faces, barely lit in the halos of light, were frozen in mixed expressions of horror and concern.

"Oh," Simon said, settling back into his seat. "But Virgil—"

"I know, Simon, you can't breathe. But you *can* breathe — there's lot of oxygen. The filter or whatever just goes down when there's no power, so it's not, like, *conditioned* air, but there's air. You can breathe. We can all breathe."

Simon nodded, trying to get his lungs to agree with what his brain told him was true. He gulped a few breaths of warm air. Then he gasped again. "The shadow-servant!" he hissed.

"What about him?" Virgil asked.

"He saw us. He saw us, and then he—and then the lights went out."

"He saw us?" Virgil asked, sounding doubtful.

"Virgil. I think he did this. I think he stopped the train…"

Virgil shook his head. "Simon, I really don't think he did. I don't even think he saw us. I was watching him the whole time, I don't think he ever turned around."

"He did," Simon insisted, "right at the end. He turned around, and he saw me. Then he stood up, and then the lights went out." A chill crawled over Simon's skin, and he shuddered. "What if he came into our car?"

"Okay, he definitely did not come into our car," Virgil said. "I know your brain, like, switched of for a second or whatever, but to come into this car, he'd have to go through that door, that door right there," he said, pointing his flashlight at the door that led to the next car. It was only a few feet away. "Trust me, Simon, if he came through that door, I'd know it."

"He saw me," Simon insisted, wiping the sweat from his brow with his sleeve. Then he remembered that he had a cell phone, too, and he pulled it out of his pocket. He turned on his flashlight and pointed it at the shadow-servant's car. But the beam wasn't strong enough to illuminate that far, and all he saw was a bright reflection that flashed in his eyes and made him see spots.

"He's sure *going* to see you if you keep shining your light at him," Virgil chided. He pushed Simon's hand down, directing the flashlight toward the floor. "The power blinks out, but it always comes back. Any second now, the lights are going to come back on, and the train—" The lights flickered back to life as he spoke, and the loud hum of the train engine revved back up in the mechanics beneath the car. The vents began to blow out filtered air, and Simon leaned his head against the glass, letting the cool breeze flutter against his burning skin. The train lurched forward and continued its slow rumbling through the open tunnel.

Simon exhaled with relief. His mind washed over with a sense of grateful calm. It was like coming up for air after being stuck in the bottom of a pool. He felt dizzy, but soothed. For a moment, the fear of the shadow-servant was obscured by the relief of light and movement. He opened his eyes, and something caught his attention outside the windows. It was difficult to get the whole picture from his angle, and the tunnel was so dark, but it looked like the tracks beneath them branched out in this wider space. Their path took them straight ahead, but the train clanked as it ran over the switch. Simon could see three other routes on this side of the train, rails that curved away from the main line. Two of the offshoot lines dead-ended almost immediately, the tracks terminating in large metal barricades that would stop the train if it was accidentally switched onto those other tracks.

But the third set of tracks disappeared into a dark tunnel. The darkness of that small space was so complete that it looked thick, like it had actual weight. The tracks didn't fade into the shadows; they disappeared abruptly at the edge of them, as if they were being swallowed up...

Simon gasped. *The shadow-servant*, he thought. He looked up, his eyes darting through the window and into the train car in front of them.

The wavy-haired man was gone.

CHAPTER 16

"I'm telling you, he stopped the train!" Simon cried. "The shadow-servant saw me, he stood up, he cut the power, and while we were all panicking in the dark, he slipped out the door and into that tunnel!"

"*You* were panicking in the dark," Virgil corrected him, sounding annoyed. "To be clear. *You* were panicking in the dark. Everyone else was great."

"He ran down that tunnel, Virg! He ran down the tunnel, and he blocked it up with his magic shadow curtain or whatever so we wouldn't see him, and wouldn't follow him." Simon crossed his arms and sat back, frustrated.

They were in the back seat of a Lyft, heading back to the Dark Matter office from the Juniata orange line stop, where they'd gotten off the train. They'd been bickering the entire time.

"Why would we follow him?" Virgil asked. "*How* would we follow him?! We were on a moving train! I don't think he was too worried that we'd bust through the windows and chase him down."

"Then where did he go?" Simon demanded. "If he didn't go down the tunnel, where did he go?"

Virgil sighed. "I'm not saying he didn't go down the tunnel. He went *somewhere*; I understand that. But I'm saying that I didn't see a 'shadow curtain' or whatever, I didn't see him turn and look at you, and you totally lost your mind down there, and it really freaked me out!"

His voice had gotten increasingly more high-pitched as he spoke. The last bit came out at a full screech. The Lyft driver raised his eyebrows at them in the rearview mirror, but said nothing.

"Sorry," Virgil mumbled to the driver.

Simon rubbed his hands down his face. He exhaled loudly and leaned his head back against the headrest. "I'm sorry," he said quietly. "I know I lost it. I've never had a panic attack before. It really freaked me out, too."

Virgil frowned. He crossed his arms and leaned against his door. "What happened to you down there?"

"I don't know," Simon said. "I'm claustrophobic, but...not usually that bad. I think it's other things, too." He rubbed his eyes. He felt so tired. "I haven't been sleeping well lately. I had the weirdest dream last night...and when I woke up, you were about to hit me with a plunger—"

"But I *didn't* hit you with a plunger," Virgil interrupted quickly.

"—and then the plates were spinning, and this whole thing with Llewyn and Morgaine, and the Shadow Lord..." He sighed, and he closed his eyes. "I don't know. I think being a wizard is frying my brain."

The Lyft driver was staring at them intently now, so incredulous that he wasn't paying attention to the road, and the car began to drift toward the shoulder. It hit the rumble strip, and the driver jerked the car back into the center of the lane. "Sorry," he said. "Sorry." But his eyes kept darting up to the rearview mirror, and his face was pale.

"First time driving wizards?" Virgil asked, giving Simon a sideways wink.

The driver cleared his throat. "Umm..." he said.

Simon looked at Virgil. Then he broke into a wide smile. "Give him a card," he said to Virgil, nodding up toward the driver. He leaned forward and said, "You never know when you might need a good Defeater of Evil or Practitioner of Kinesthetic Magic."

Virgil laughed and handed the driver a card, relieved to have broken the tension with his best friend.

"So what do we do now?" Simon asked. "We lost the shadow-servant, so the whole time travel thing was a total waste."

"Yeah...man. If he *did* see you, I wonder how badly we messed up the timeline."

"Well, the good news is, there's no way for us to know how it would have gone otherwise, so we definitely can't ever say that we made it worse," Simon said.

"But we did lose our only lead," Virgil frowned. "So what *do* we do? Sit back and wait for the Shadow Lord to attack us again?"

"That's an option," Simon said, nodding slowly. "But I think I have a better idea."

Virgil's eyes narrowed suspiciously. "What's that?" he asked.

Simon set his lips into a hard line. "I think it's time we went on the offensive."

CHAPTER 17

"*This* is 'going on the offensive'?" Virgil asked.

They were sitting in the Pontiac, stopped dead in bumper-to-bumper traffic on the interstate.

"I didn't say it would be a fast and furious offensive," Simon pointed out.

Virgil shook his head. "I find rush hour *very* furiously offensive."

Simon's plan was simple enough, and it revolved around the fact that the shadow-servant hadn't actually been their only lead. They also had the information they'd gotten from Templario, the mysterious Redditor.

"But why would he send us a list of old people who defected to the Shadow Lord and tried to drain my youthful good looks? We already *know* that old people defected to the Shadow Lord and tried to drain my youthful good looks, and we already put a stop to it."

"And, unless the mail got really held up, we put a stop to it *before* Templario sent us the paperwork," Simon added.

"Yeah, that's weird," Virgil agreed, musing over the facts. "Why would he send us a clue about what was happening after we already *solved* what was happening?"

"Maybe he didn't. Maybe it *did* get lost in the mail for a week."

"Or maybe it's not even a real list. Maybe it was planted by the shadow-servant."

"I don't know why he'd give us something to throw us off the trail of a problem we already solved," Simon pointed out. He rubbed his forehead, trying to keep an oncoming headache at bay. The whole situation was like putting together a puzzle when all the pieces were flipped over, face-down. "Besides, I think the mail he brought was legit. Not the shadow trap, obviously, but the ads and everything...I've gotten those ads before. He might have faked them, but I don't know why he'd go to the trouble."

"Yeah, and he tossed that mail bag into the alley," Virgil said, suddenly remembering. "It looked pretty full. Like it was a real mailman's real bag."

Simon tried hard not to dwell on what might have happened to the mail bag's original carrier. It made him sick to his stomach just thinking about the possibilities. He pushed those thoughts down and tried to focus on the problem at hand. "So assuming it was a real letter sent by the real Templario, it either got stuck in the mail for a while, or else the retirement homes are still at play in the Shadow Lord's plan somehow."

"We could look at the postmark," Virgil suggested. "That'd tell us when it was mailed."

"It would," Simon agreed, "if the envelope hadn't been sucked into the shadow vortex."

Virgil frowned. "Oh, yeah."

"But the other thing we know from Templario—or at least, the other thing that Templario says—is that Furtive Hills really exists, and that it's somewhere in the valley beyond the Stocks. We find Furtive Hills, we find the Shadow Lord's army—and maybe the Shadow Lord himself."

"If we can ever get through this traffic," Virgil grumbled.

"If we can ever get through this traffic," Simon agreed.

They inched forward, moving at a glacial pace along the 85. But the off-ramp to the 110 was in sight, and once they made it there, it would be clear sailing into the Bypass Mountains.

Something was bothering Virgil. "I like this new proactive approach, but why aren't we waiting until Llewyn is stitched back together, or whatever? Wouldn't it be good to have a real wizard on our side? Especially now that it sounds like Morgaine separated out the dark blade? We could charge in with the full power of a Serpent-Order Kindle mage."

"Seventh Order Kinesthetic mage," Simon corrected him.

"Why don't we wait until we have him back?"

Simon took a deep breath. He wondered how many challenging conversations they could possibly have in one twenty-four-hour period. "I've been thinking of that," he said slowly, trying to approach the topic with tact. "I think we might have to accept the fact that Morgaine isn't on our side, and that there's a very real chance that she's not even actually helping Llewyn."

Virgil screwed up his face in confusion. "But she said—"

"I know what she said," Simon replied, cutting him off, "but think about it. She purposefully shattered him, then she floated off with all the pieces. Who knows where she brought them, and all we know since then is that she said he's slowly being stitched together, and that he's going to be fine, and then she changed the subject." Simon tightened his grip on the steering wheel as he eased the car forward. "Virgil...I think there's a real possibility that Llewyn might not be coming back."

Virgil opened his mouth, but no words came out. He closed it again, and he turned in his seat, facing front and watching the slow roll of the cars ahead, lost deeply in thought. Finally, he said, "I think you might be right."

"You do?" Simon asked, surprised. He had expected some sort of glass-half-full pushback from Virgil.

"Yeah. We should have never set Morgaine free," Virgil said quietly, staring out the window. "I know it looks like Llewyn trusted her, but you're right...she's not on our side, and she's too powerful to be trusted." He turned and looked Simon in the eye. "Abby should never have summoned her."

Simon started. "Well...it's not *Abby's* fault. She followed Llewyn's instructions, it was all three of us who decided to set her free."

Virgil shrugged. "I don't know. I'm just saying, Morgaine's a potential problem that we're going to have to deal with, and she's a problem we wouldn't have if Abby hadn't summoned her."

Simon furrowed his brow. "Okay..." he said slowly, chewing over his words before he said them. "This conversation took a sharp turn I didn't expect. Let's just...focus on finding Furtive Hills, and we'll try to avoid direct contact with the Shadow Lord if we can."

"Okay," Virgil said. He slumped down in his seat, propped his feet up on the dashboard, and leaned his head against the passenger window, gazing out at the mountainous landscape to the south.

A few minutes later, they had inched forward far enough to break out of the lane and onto the ramp that took them toward the Stocks. But before he turned off, while they were still sitting in traffic, Simon quietly slipped his phone from his pocket and sent Abby a text:

Something's up with Virgil. Something's wrong.

CHAPTER 18

It was past noon by the time they reached the bottom of the Stocks, and Simon was wishing that he'd thought to stop for lunch. "You hungry?" he asked Virgil. It was the first time either of them had spoken since they had gotten out of traffic.

"Nah," Virgil said, staring out the window.

That's a first, Simon thought. Virgil was always hungry.

"Everything okay?" Simon asked, trying to keep the question casual, despite the fact that he had a small knot of dread gnawing at his stomach.

Virgil looked over and gave him a quizzical look. "Everything's fine," he said, sounding confused. Then he turned back to the window and watched the mountains roll past.

The silence felt a little too heavy, so Simon clicked on the radio.

The Pontiac was too old to have a CD player, and the tape deck had busted a few years earlier. The antenna had gone wonky, too, and the radio only got a handful of stations, and even those were usually pretty fuzzy with static.

But static was better than silence just then.

The sound popped and fizzled through the speakers, some old country song that Simon had never heard. He pushed the buttons to check the other stations, but nothing else came in this deep into the Bypass Mountains, so he settled on the scratchy country. But just as he cycled back to it, the song ended, and the DJ broke back in: "We'll be back with more classic country hits, right after this news break."

"News *again*," Virgil said, rolling his eyes. But Simon held up a hand for quiet.

"Grimsley Manor is still missing," the news anchor informed them, "and investigators are no closer to figuring out where it's gone. Peter Grimsley, who is still in Pittsburgh, has not been reached for comment."

"If my house disappeared, I probably wouldn't come home either," Virgil shrugged.

The anchor continued. "The Templar Mayor's Office today has announced a new budget that will allow for long sought-after repairs and upgrades to the Templar commuter system."

"They're fixing the subway?" Simon asked, surprised.

Virgil straightened up in his seat. "Guess they really want to work for that Simon Dark transit money after all." He reached over and turned up the volume.

"According to the Mayor's Office, the money has been ear-marked for new buses, and for new railcars for the green, yellow, gray, and red lines. The orange line will be slated for budgetary review when transit is back on the docket in three more years."

Simon gaped down at the radio. "You're not updating the orange line?" he cried. "Have you *seen* the orange line lately?!"

"Just this morning, in fact," Virgil replied.

"Not you—them! *Them!*" Simon slapped the dashboard a couple of times, and the radio lost power. He drew his hand back. "Whoops..."

"Eh. That radio had it coming," Virgil said.

Simon returned his hand to the wheel and navigated them up the steep slope of the Stocks. "Man," he said, shaking his head in disbelief. "How is it possible that they can have money for every single train *except* the orange line?"

"And new buses, too," Virgil reminded him. "We just got new buses, like, four years ago." He scoffed. "Your tax dollars at work, Simon."

"Yours, too," Simon frowned.

Virgil rubbed his chin. "Did I remember to pay taxes this year...?" he asked, honestly unsure.

Simon sighed. "Everything about everything feels like it's just a few degrees off today," he said, mostly to himself.

Virgil screwed up his face in confusion. "What does that mean?" he asked.

"It means everything has been just a little off all day, and I can't put my finger on why, or how, but there's something that's knocking everything off its axis." He rubbed his eyes with one hand while he guided them over the rise of the Stocks and turned the car down toward the valley below. "Or maybe I just need more sleep."

"Well, warn me if you're going to nod off behind the wheel," Virgil said. "And whatever you're going to do, do it fast." He pointed through the windshield at the valley below. A thick blanket of fog covered the hillside, completely obscuring the bottom of the valley. A few hundred yards down the slope, the highway disappeared into the murky grey cloud, and it didn't appear again until it was halfway up the next mountain, far in the distance. "Things are about to get Furtive."

The car plunged into the valley, and Simon and Virgil were swallowed up by the fog.

CHAPTER 19

"I can't see anything," Virgil complained.

"I think that's the point," Simon whispered, trying to hold back a shudder.

The fog was dense, thicker than they had ever seen. It wrapped around the car like a blanket, and Simon had to slow down or else risk running off the road. He could only see two feet in front of the car.

"How are we supposed to find the turnoff in all this?" Virgil said.

"I think that's the point, too."

They eased slowly down the mountain. It was otherworldly, driving through the thick, cottony mist. They felt suddenly and completely isolated from the world. Even the sound of the car's motor was deadened by the wall of vapor, and they passed almost silently through the cloud.

"We could pull over and get out...walk around until we find it," Virgil said, but it was a half-hearted suggestion at best.

"I don't want to leave the car on the side of the road," Simon replied. "Also, I'm honestly not sure we'd ever find our way back."

The mountain highway wound down toward the valley, and Simon had to keep both hands on the wheel and both eyes on the road in order to keep the car on track. "We'll never find it like this. We have to cut through the fog."

"How do we do that?" Virgil asked.

Simon thought for a few moments as he piloted the car around a bend. "We could try burning it off," he finally suggested.

"Fog burns?" Virgil asked, confused.

Simon sighed. "It's a figure of speech," he said. "If you heat it up, it evaporates."

"Oh," Virgil said. Then he frowned. "So you're saying we need to make the sun come out." It had been cloudy all week, and the sun hadn't made many appearances in the last few days.

"I'm saying that maybe we could use some kinesthetic heat to burn a hole in the fog."

"Oh!" Virgil said, brightening. But then his face fell again. "But our magic's not, like, *hot*."

"But maybe we can *make* it hot."

"I don't know..." Virgil said doubtfully.

"Well, I didn't know if I could grow shotgun plants or ladder-web threads with my magic, but lo and behold..." Simon pointed out.

Virgil nodded slowly. "That's a good point," he admitted. "All right. Let's give it a shot."

He rolled down the passenger window and stuck one arm outside of the car. He took a few deep breaths to center himself, then he pushed his energy into the palm of his hand. Thin streaks of orange light flowed down his arm and gathered in his palm, and the usual orange ball began to form...but he focused on the light, willing the kinesthetic energy to take a different form, imagining hot, dry desert air and the scorching blast from an opened oven. The orange color faded from the magic in his hand, and the kinesthetic ball became transparent, with heat lines waving in the air above his palm. He felt a sudden warmth against the skin of his hand.

"I did it!" he cried.

"Good!" Simon nodded encouragingly. "Now use it."

Virgil extended his arm farther out into the open air, and he pushed the hot energy out from his palm. The wavy heat lines extended into the fog, and bits of the mist turned to steam and melted away like cotton candy. Suddenly, they could see the edge of the road, and a few inches of grass beyond the shoulder.

"Can you point it ahead of the car?" Simon asked.

Virgil swung his arm around toward the front and pushed harder. The line of heat streamed from his palm like water from a hose, stretching out into the mountainside, burning through the fog and giving them a clear view of the land several yards past the edge of the road.

"Good!" Simon said. "Keep it up!"

"What if the driveway's on the other side of the road?" Virgil asked.

"Then we'll turn around and come back up the other way."

They continued on down the highway with Virgil clearing a path through the fog ahead of the car, and to the right. Simon picked up speed, now that he had a little more visibility, but they still weren't going very fast.

"Uh, think we could pick it up a little more?" Virgil asked, frowning down at his hand.

"Not without running off the road," Simon replied. "Why?"

Beads of sweat began to form on Virgil's forehead, and a sheen of perspiration coated his arm. "Because this thing is starting to burn."

The skin on Virgil's palm was turning pink from the heat of the magic. It had started out feeling just sort of warm, like he was holding a fresh biscuit, but the longer he held the magic and the harder he pushed it out into the fog, the more intense the heat became.

"Simon," he said, his voice starting to get high with panic, "go faster!"

"I can't!" Simon cried.

"My hand is burning!"

"I'm going as fast as I can!"

"It hurts!" Virgil yelled.

"Then stop doing it!" Simon said.

"But we need to find the road!"

"Then stop complaining!"

"But it *hurts!*" Virgil whined.

Simon shouted in frustration and pushed his foot down on the gas. The Pontiac picked up speed, and the road came at them fast. The highway curved to the right, and another car burst out from the fog coming in the other direction, flashing its lights and honking its horn. Simon jerked the wheel, just barely hugging the edge of his lane as the car careened around the curve.

"I can't hold it!" Virgil screamed. His face was red, his hair was matted down with sweat, and small blisters had begun to bubble up on his palm. "Simon!"

"There!" Simon cried. He saw a flash of a rock road leading off to the right. He pulled the wheel, and the Pontiac screeched off the highway, hitting the gravel road hard, slamming down and bottoming out on the shoulder. The tires screeched as Simon slammed on the brakes, and the Pontiac skidded at an angle, the back tires throwing rocks everywhere as the car fishtailed into the grass.

They rocked to a sudden stop. Simon's knuckles were white on the wheel. Virgil pulled his hand inside the window, shook out the heat-magic, and blew on his palm, wincing in pain.

"You could have stopped," Simon said.

Virgil flexed his fingers, testing the extent of his burns. "That's not what heroes do," he said. The blisters didn't look as bad or as angry now that the heat was off of his hand. His palm stung like crazy, but he decided he could live with the pain. "I wonder if Furtive Hills has any ice," he said miserably, blowing cool air onto the burns. "I need to learn a healing spell when Llewyn is—" He stopped himself before he could finish the thought. He looked over at Simon guiltily.

Simon tried to smile. "Hey, maybe he really *will* be okay," he said, trying to sound positive.

"Well, anyway," Virgil said, changing the subject, "we found the driveway." He peered outside the car. Without the benefit of his kinesthetic heat, the fog had closed back in around them, and they could no longer even see the highway just a few feet behind them. "Now what do we do?"

"I guess we go see what we can see," Simon said.

He pulled the car off the gravel road, driving it slowly into the grass a few yards away so that it was hidden from both the highway and the driveway by the fog. Then they got out and started walking deeper into the fog, staying in the grass, keeping the gravel path just in sight.

"Remind me what our game plan is here?" Virgil asked as they trudged through the mist.

"I think our main objective is to see what Furtive Hills even *is*. And to get an idea of what sort of army the Shadow Lord is building."

"That's two objectives," Virgil pointed out.

"Don't be pedantic," Simon said, rolling his eyes.

"I don't know what that word means," Virgil said proudly. "And I'd like to suggest a third objective: to not die."

"That's a pretty good one," Simon admitted.

The air was chilly, made colder by the dampness of the fog, and Simon zipped up his jacket. Virgil didn't seem to mind; he left his jacket open, even though he was only wearing a short-sleeve T-shirt beneath it. Maybe he was just still hot from the kinesthetic fog-burning. But Simon couldn't help but find it strange as he shivered against the chill.

He snuck a peek at his phone. Abby hadn't responded to his text.

The mountainside was deathly silent as they pushed on, and it was impossible to tell how far they'd gone; the fog obscured all sense of time and place. Simon couldn't help but feel claustrophobic again as they walked through the dense mist, and he worked to push down his panic, to keep it contained to the pit of his stomach...but the deeper into the valley they went, the more his skin began to prickle.

"There," Virgil said suddenly, pointing through the fog.

There was a break in the cloud up ahead, as if the vapor ran up against an invisible fence and stopped dead outside the perimeter of Furtive Hills—which, Simon supposed, made sense; the fog was a cloaking mechanism, but it wouldn't do much good for the people living and working for the Shadow Lord if they couldn't see anything.

Simon and Virgil could see through the edge of the barrier, to a tall, wide, brick-and-stone building that rose up before them like a sleeping giant. It was a massive, sprawling structure, with several stories, arched doorways, and sculpted parapets, with two turrets like a castle, stretching up toward the sky, and with a handful of tall stone chimneys belching out steady curls of wood smoke.

Virgil tilted his head, scrutinizing the enormous house. "Does it look sort of familiar to you?" he asked, squinting through the fog.

"It does," Simon said slowly, trying to place the building in his memory. He felt like he had just seen it somewhere recently, but he couldn't quite remember where...

And then it clicked for both of them at the same time. They had seen the building that very morning, in photographs on the news.

There, looming in the middle of the fog, in the valley on the far side of the Stocks, stood the missing Grimsley Manor.

CHAPTER 20

"Peter Grimsley is the Shadow Lord?!" Virgil hissed, incredulous.

But Simon shook his head. "I seriously doubt the playboy millionaire heir of the Grimsley fortune is an ultra-dimensional shadow creature sent to destroy Templar," he said. "I think he just happened to have a house big enough to hold the Shadow Lord's army, and the Shadow Lord swiped it while Grimsley was out of town."

Virgil exhaled slowly, puffing up his cheeks and blowing out the air through pursed lips. "Well, bright side: the Shadow Lord's army can fit inside a single house."

"Downside: it's big enough that it fits into *that* single house," Simon countered.

There was movement near the front of the house, and they instinctively retreated into the fog. They skirted around to their left, keeping low to the ground and crouching behind a hillock as the front door to the mansion opened, and two tall, broad men in headsets stepped out into the gravel drive. They wore loose-fitting purple canvas robes with the same yellow circle-and-triangle design they had seen on the man named Leonard who set up the Refracticore in the woods the week before.

Their hands glowed with a strange purple light.

They took up positions on either side of the front door, standing like pillars. The guard on the left clapped his hands together, and the sharp shock of it echoed across the clearing, dying as it reached the mist. He pulled his hands back apart, and as he did, a long, black staff appeared, growing in length as he spread his palms. When it was about four feet long, the guard turned his hands and gripped the staff by its center. An electric purple light appeared around the edges, flowing out to the ends of the staff until the whole thing glowed with magical energy.

The second guard followed suit, going through the same motions, and pulling a glowing staff from the space between his own hands. He gave it a twirl, spinning it a few times, creating an electric purple circle in the air.

"Shadow staffs," Virgil breathed, transfixed by the glowing black and purple weapons.

Simon gave him a look. "How do you always know what things are called?" he asked. "Shadow Lord, shadow trap, shadow staffs…"

"It's easy," Virgil insisted. "You figure out what it is, then you put 'shadow' in front of it."

Simon blinked. "Oh," he said.

"I'm surprised you didn't pick up on that right way. But then again, I, unlike you, pay attention," Virgil said smugly.

"Yeah, yeah," Simon grumbled.

They watched the guards for a few minutes, and it became clear that they had no intention of leaving their post, at least not any time soon. "Think we can take them?" Virgil asked.

"I think it's possible, depending on what their weapons are capable of. And depending on if it's just the weapons that are magic, or if the guards themselves have shadow-magic. If it's just the weapons, we can probably knock them out with a few energy blasts."

"Or with Gladys," Virgil said, smiling at the memory of knocking out Leonard on the Stocks.

"Right. But if the guards themselves have powers—and it looks like they probably do, with those glowing hands—then I don't know." Simon sighed. "I'm guessing they're not guards for no reason."

Virgil looked around, examining the front of the mansion. "All right," he said, pointing to a smaller portico near the far end of the mansion. "Let's try another door."

They snuck through the fog, on what should have been a short trek to the side of the mansion. But the manor was larger than it looked, and although they were walking so quickly they were almost running, it was almost five full minutes before they were lined up with the portico near the end of the building. By the time they got there, they were both out of breath.

Simon dropped to one knee, panting and wiping the sweat from his forehead. "No good," he wheezed, nodding over at the columns that formed the front of the portico. "Look."

There were two more guards blocking those doors, one man and one woman, both clad in the same purple canvas robes, and both holding black shadow staffs that gave off the same electric purple glow.

Virgil groaned. He crouched down, planting his hands on the ground and trying to catch his breath. "Well. We could try around back..."

Simon snorted. "It'd be dark by the time we got there," he said. "Besides, if both these doors are guarded, I'm sure *all* the doors are guarded."

"Then what do we do?" Virgil fretted. "We need to know what we're up against. We *have* to get inside that house."

A thoughtful smile spread slowly across Simon's face. "If we can't find a door that's far away from the guards...then maybe we can get the guards far away from the doors."

He placed both hands on the cool, damp ground so that his palms were flat against the grass. He closed his eyes, focused his energies, and pushed streams of orange light deep into the earth. Then he lifted his fingers, urging the magic forward, and

Virgil could just barely make out a trace of a light trail moving from Simon's hands toward Grimsley Manor.

"What are you doing?" Virgil whispered.

"Trying something," Simon muttered back without opening his eyes. And that was all he said; he shifted his entire focus on the magic happening beneath the surface.

The faded light trail sped across the grounds, hitting the house just a few feet away from the guards standing at attention on the portico. But whatever magic Simon had conjured didn't appear to be targeting the manor itself, at least not in a way that was immediately visible to Virgil. The light trail dissipated, like the fading streak of a shooting star, without the guards even registering its existence. But Simon held the heels of his palms against the earth and still appeared to be channeling his magic deep into the ground.

"Simon," Virgil said, and he shifted his weight from one foot to the other uncomfortably. "What's happening?"

But Simon didn't reply. His focus was completely locked on the magic he was pushing through the earth.

Virgil looked nervously up at the guards, but they still hadn't noticed the light of the magic trail, and now it was completely faded away, so there was nothing to be worried about, at least in that respect. But Virgil couldn't help but frown at the thought of how Simon had grown plants that shot orange balls of magic while he, Virgil, was imprisoned by the energy beam on the Stocks, and how Simon had created a ladder-web to escape the shadow trap earlier that very day, when Llewyn hadn't taught them either of those spells. Simon's power was growing, it was changing; it was evolving faster than Virgil's, and without the aid of their mystic guide.

Everything about it made Virgil nervous.

A little envious, too. But mostly, nervous.

He was about to tell Simon that maybe they should try to find another method of getting inside the manor when suddenly, both guards put their hands to their earpieces and listened to some secret command coming in over the airwaves.

Something was happening.

The guards turned and ran back into the house, crashing through the portico doors and not even stopping to close them.

Virgil mentally corrected himself. It wasn't just that something was happening.

It was that something *big* was happening.

"Simon?" he asked, bewildered. He turned and peered over at the guards who stood by the main doors, and they, too, had disappeared back into the mansion. He heard a few distant shouts coming from inside the building.

Virgil turned and looked down at Simon, his eyes wide with concern. "Simon," he said, "what did you do?"

Simon opened his eyes. He blinked a few times, as if he were disoriented and trying to get his bearings. He looked up at Virgil quizzically, and then a look of recognition washed over his face. He lifted his hands from the grass and wiped them on his jeans. "I think I made a sinkhole in the backyard," he replied. He stood up and brushed the grass from his knees. "I couldn't see where the magic was going, with the house in the way, but a sinkhole in the backyard is what I was trying for." He squinted toward the house, searching for the guards and finding only open doors instead. "I guess I made *something* happen back there," he said with a shrug. Then he headed toward the house. "Come on."

They pushed through the fog and broke into the clearing around the mansion. The act of breaking into the open space reminded them both of the booby trap the Shadow Lord had set for them in the clearing on the Stocks, and as soon as they stepped into the grass, they stopped, skidding to a halt and looking around for another mud-miner—or something worse—to break through the ground. But there was no sound of shattering glass, and nothing pushed through the dirt, and after a few moments of collecting themselves, it became clear that the mansion wasn't protected by magical tripwires.

They both exhaled with relief, then they pushed forward, sprinting toward the house.

CHAPTER 21

Virgil peeked his head inside the mansion. "Hello?"

"Don't say 'hello' when we're trying to sneak in!" Simon hissed, swatting Virgil on the shoulder.

"Sorry," Virgil muttered. "Just checking for henchmen."

Luckily, there was no one inside the mansion's great foyer, and Simon and Virgil managed to slip in undetected.

"How long do you think a sinkhole will keep the guards busy?" Virgil asked.

"I have no idea," Simon admitted. "So I think we should move fast."

They jogged across the entryway and ducked into the first room they found, a grand living area with animal-skin rugs and soft leather couches surrounding a fire pit that was set into the floor in the center of the room, with its smoke stack leading straight up to the middle of the ceiling. There was a fire crackling in the fireplace, and divots on a few of the couch cushions from the people who had been sitting there only moments before.

It was anyone's guess when those people would be back.

Simon and Virgil dashed out of the room and moved deeper into the enormous house. "What are we looking for?" Virgil whispered as they dodged from one opulent room to the next.

"Anything that looks like a bunker, or a mess hall, or a training room…I don't know, anything that looks *military*," Simon said, and his own uncertainty made his voice come out in a harsh whisper. "We're looking for an army."

They ran past a kitchen, and a dining room, and a game room, and a study, peeking in as they moved, looking for something, *anything* that might mark the house as a base for an evil shadow-army...but every room was just a standard, run-of-the-mill room in a house made for a millionaire.

As they tore past the study, Virgil skidded to a stop, his sneakers screeching on the polished wood floor. Simon winced at the sound of it, but the guards were still preoccupied, it seemed, and no one came running.

Virgil retraced his steps and poked his head into the study. "Look," he said.

Simon peeked in over Virgil's shoulder. The room was enormous and exquisite, with oak bookshelves built into the walls, filled with hardcover books, and not a single one of them looked to have been published within the last hundred years. There was another fireplace in this room, set into the exterior wall, but this one was cold and dark, clean and completely devoid of logs and ash. No one had built a fire in this room for some time.

"Wow," Simon said, stepping into the space. Almost immediately, he saw what had captured Virgil's attention. The fireplace was flanked by two massive floor-to-ceiling windows that looked out over the backyard of the mountainside estate. Simon walked up close to one of the windows and marveled at the scene outside.

"Holy Hamburg," Virgil breathed, taking in the chaos that was occurring in the yard. "I guess your sinkhole worked."

The field out beyond the back side of the mansion stretched for half a mile at least before it disappeared into another wall of dense fog up the hill, near the southern horizon. It was an impressively expansive swath of land that stood treeless and empty between the mansion and the mist.

And nearly every single square foot of it had fallen into a massive hole in the earth.

The circular pit in the yard started just a few yards from the back of the house and extended even beyond the barrier of mist, the far end of the hole obscured by the roiling fog that hung thickly in the air and pooled downward into the bottom of the hole. From side to side, the sinkhole was almost as wide as the house, which meant that all together, the pit was about the size of a full city block.

The hole was so deep that they couldn't see the bottom of it, even though the ground sloped away from the back of the house, and they had a pretty good view of its depth. There must have been people who fell down into the hole when it opened, because the mansion's guards were lowering ropes down into the pit and waving their hands wildly. The gravel driveway had split off in the front of the house and curled around to the back, leading to a garage or a parking area, or *something* back behind the house, but that parking area, along with whatever vehicles had been parked there, had also sunk down into the pit. A steady stream of rocks spilled over the edge of the sinkhole, marking the place where the driveway had run, and the familiar white van with FURTIVE HILLS painted on the outside was teetering precariously on the edge of it, threatening to tip down into the earth as a small crew of shadow-guards grabbed onto the bumper and tried to pull it back onto solid ground.

Simon and Virgil stared out at the sinkhole, incredulous. Simon looked down slowly at his hands, mesmerized by their power. "Guess I'll keep that one in the repertoire," he muttered in amazement.

"This...isn't actually what I wanted you to see when I brought us into this room," Virgil said, sounding dazed, gaping at the melee outside the window. He reluctantly tore his eyes away from the scene and jerked his thumb toward the other side of the room. "I meant *that*."

Simon looked over and saw what Virgil was gesturing toward. One of the bookcases was opened at an angle, one end of it jutting out into the room.

"A secret door," Simon said, tilting his head at the bookcase. "Oh."

"Yeah," Virgil said, clearing his throat. "It was...it was more impressive before. Before we...saw the sinkhole." He coughed, and cleared his throat again.

"No, no, it's still good," Simon said encouragingly. "It's a great lead. Really..." He let his eyes wander back over to the massive circular hole in the backyard. "It's really good," he said quietly.

Virgil exhaled awkwardly. "Well, it's...something we should probably check. Right?" he asked, heading toward the open bookcase.

"Definitely—yeah, yeah," Simon agreed, peeling himself away from the window. He gave his head a shake and worked to re-focus his attention. "A secret passageway is a good place to look for a secret army."

They passed behind the bookcase and found a set of wooden stairs leading down to a lower level. Virgil went first, poking his head around the corner. When he saw that the coast was clear, he stepped onto the stairwell and began to ease himself down slowly, with Simon close behind him.

The steps led down to another secret panel, which had also been left ajar. Virgil cautiously pushed it all the way open and stepped out into a wide hallway with a polished wooden floor. If the panel concealing the staircase had been closed, it would have appeared to be just the end of the hallway.

Simon followed Virgil out into the secret floor and took in the view of the corridor. "This hallway alone is bigger than our entire apartment," he muttered, shaking his head.

There were chandeliers hanging from the ceiling, and ornate sconces set into the walls every few yards, giving the space a bright but cozy glow. The hallway turned at a hard angle after about thirty yards, veering off to another section of the unbelievably large house. There were a handful of doorways set into the walls, but none of them actually had doors. They were just empty portals into additional rooms, and each opening had a brass plaque next to it explaining what the room was.

"It's like a museum down here," said Virgil.

"A museum that no one is supposed to see," added Simon.

They stepped cautiously down the hallway, trying not to make too much noise with their footfalls. Virgil's sneaker squeaked on the hardwood floor—again—and Simon winced—again. They froze, listening to see if anyone was coming. They were about to carry on silently when their ears picked up the sound of footsteps heading their way, and fast.

Simon grabbed Virgil by the arm and pulled him into the open doorway on their left. The room was dark, and they dove into the shadows just as three women in purple canvas robes rushed by. One of the women slapped her hand against the false wall panel, and it opened at her touch. They ducked into the secret room and ran up the stairs.

Neither Simon nor Virgil moved for a full thirty seconds.

Finally, when he was sure the coast was clear, Virgil whispered, "Boy. That was close."

Simon looked around the room in which they found themselves. There was a long, dark hallway leading to the main room, and there was light filtering into the space, even though the lights in the room itself were turned off. They could see a dim, watery glow from around the corner of the entryway. Simon crept up to the edge of the wall and looked into the heart of the room.

He gasped.

The room was set up like a movie theater, with folding chairs arranged on risers that formed a semi-circle around a curved glass window. The window itself was massive, reaching from the floor to the ceiling, and from one wall to the other. It looked out over a horrifying scene.

"Virgil," he whispered, motioning his friend over. "You have to see this."

The room below the viewing area was an operating room, something straight out of a mid-century sanitarium. The floor was laid with small white tiles that sloped downward into a drain that was set in the very center of the floor. There were stainless steel cabinets along the walls, and through the reinforced glass in the cabinet doors, Simon could see scalpels, clamps, saws, forceps, spreaders, and a lot more medical equipment that he couldn't identify.

The door leading into the room below was heavy steel with a circular porthole window in the center, and next to that, hanging on the wall, was a rolled-up garden hose with a spray nozzle fitted onto the end.

The watery light that filtered into the seating area came from a set of lights positioned over the center of the operating room that had been dimmed down to their lowest setting, bathing the white-tile space in an eerie blue glow.

"You won't believe it," Simon murmured, mesmerized and horrified by the sight.

"Is it an operating theatre?" Virgil asked.

Simon furrowed his brow. He turned back and looked questioningly at his friend. "How did you know?" he asked.

Virgil pointed up at the brass plate screwed into the wall at the entrance from the main hallway. The words OPERATING THEATER were stamped into the metal. "I pay attention," he said.

Virgil padded down the dark entryway into the theatre, joining Simon behind the back row of seats. "Wow," he said, looking down into the space. "I've seen some creepy things in my life. And this is definitely one of them."

"At what point in the Grimsley history did the family house require an operating room?" Simon murmured, wondering out loud.

"It could be worse. At least it's not in use," Virgil said.

As if on cue, the door of the operating room opened, and the lights increased in intensity as two people in doctor's scrubs walked in.

Simon and Virgil instinctively crouched down, though the viewing space was still dark, and it would have been almost impossible for the people below to see them.

The doctors, one female and one male, wore surgical caps on their heads and masks over their noses and mouths. They stepped into the room with their gloved hands held up in the air, bent at the elbows, avoiding direct contact with any surfaces. They moved toward the middle of the room, and one of the doctors set to work unlocking the various cabinets. She plucked out a handful of tools and placed them all on a metal pan. Meanwhile, the other doctor crooked his fingers at the wall on the other side of the room, as if beckoning someone forward. A panel in the wall slid up, disappearing into the ceiling and revealing a narrow door through which a third doctor wheeled in a broad, powerful-looking brunette woman who was strapped to a gurney. She was wearing a hospital gown; thick bands at her knees, her hips, and her chest held her securely down on the metal cart. She was conscious, but just barely; the doctor who wheeled her in was also towing an IV stand that was attached to the patient's arm by way of a needle that was dripping anesthesia into her system.

The doctors appeared to be talking to each other, but Simon and Virgil couldn't hear anything from the theatre room. It was then that Simon noticed a thin microphone hanging down from the center of the light fixture. It would be possible to hear everything in the viewing room, but only if the mic was turned on.

They watched in silence as the third doctor wheeled the gurney to the center of the room, over the drain in the floor, and then retreated back through the narrow doorway. The panel slid back down behind her, leaving the two surgeons alone in the operating space with the patient.

"I don't think I want to watch a surgery," Virgil said, the color draining from his face.

"I don't think I do, either," Simon agreed. But neither of them made any move to leave the room.

The male doctor gripped the patient's right hand and slid a hard foam pad beneath it, propping it up on the gurney. He retrieved a red marker that was clipped to the collar of his scrubs and drew circles around three of her knuckles, where her first, middle, and ring fingers met her hand. Then he repeated the process with her other hand, taking care not to dislodge the needle in her arm.

When he was done making his marks, he nodded at the female doctor. They chatted back and forth for a minute or two, the fabric of their masks fluttering with the movement of their lips. Then the female doctor picked up a scalpel, positioned herself next to the gurney, and began to slice open the patient's knuckles, carving quick but careful circles along the red markings.

"Oh, I'm going to be sick," Virgil said, clamping a hand over his mouth.

"We should go," Simon said.

But still, neither of them moved.

"Hey. Look at that," Simon said, pointing down into the theater.

Virgil peeked through the viewing window. "What am I looking for?" he asked.

"Notice anything weird about the shadows?"

Virgil squinted down at the scene below. "*Which* shadows?" he asked, confused.

Simon nodded. "Exactly."

And then Virgil understood. The gurney and the shelves had dark shadows in the glaring brightness of the light fixture, but neither of the doctors cast shadows themselves.

"Why don't the doctors have shadow?" Simon asked, alarmed.

"I don't know, but it seriously creeps me out," Virgil whispered.

As the surgeon was finishing her initial cuts on the patient's hand, the door in the wall slid open again, and the third doctor reemerged, this time carrying a tray with a blue towel thrown over it. Whatever was hiding on the tray was glowing a lime green color, its light diffused through the thin blue material of the towel.

And, they couldn't help but notice, the tray itself threw a shadow onto the floor, but the doctor carrying the tray did not.

The surgeon making the cuts motioned to the third doctor with a shake of her head; the doctor brought the tray over to the gurney. The surgeon picked up the towel, carefully folding it back, and revealed the contents of the tray.

There were six small stones sitting on the metal, radiating their bright green light from within their centers.

"What...*are* those?" Simon murmured, craning his neck to try to get a better look.

"Maybe we should go," Virgil said, and this time he actually did take a few steps backward, toward the entrance to the room. His face was white as a sheet, and he looked as if he might pass out.

"Hold on," Simon said, leaning forward. "I want to see this..."

He watched as the surgeon used a pair of tweezers to pick up one of the small stones. Using her free hand, she snatched up the scalpel and used the flat edge of it to lift up the flap of skin that covered one of the patient's exposed knuckles. Then she carefully set the green stone onto the bone, took a few seconds to position it just right, and laid the flap of skin back over it. The green glow of the stone was bright through the patient's skin, and even the smear of blood that coated her hand couldn't dull the sickly green shine.

The surgeon repeated the process on each of the patient's exposed knuckles. Then she moved around and started working on the other hand. Meanwhile, the male surgeon took up the space at the patient's completed hand and began sewing up her knuckles, using a fine thread to stitch the flap back to the skin of her hand.

In less than ten minutes, the whole horrible procedure was complete. The patient had six glowing-green knuckles now, three on each hand. The third doctor began wrapping her wounds with gauze, and while she worked, the other two surgeons backed out of the main door, nodding and chattering away as they left the operating room.

"Simon, can we please go?" Virgil pleaded. He had backed almost all the way out of the room.

Simon nodded slowly. "Yeah," he said. He tore his eyes away from the operating room and joined Virgil in the darkened hall.

"Why did they do that to her?" Virgil asked, and his forehead as covered by a wet sheen. He took a few deep breaths, trying to calm the awful roiling in his stomach.

"I have no idea," Simon said, shaking his head.

He stepped out into the main hallway, shuffling as if in a daze, trying to process what he had just witnessed.

Which was why he didn't notice the bright blue light that exploded against his temple, slamming his skull against the wall, and knocking him to the ground, unconscious.

CHAPTER 22

Simon was back in the dark-sky place.

The green and pink and blue lights flickered and flashed across the darkness overhead, and the ground was spongy beneath his feet. There was no trace of the red, viscous flood.

He had that same sense of being on both ends of a horizon at once.

And he still felt like he was standing up sideways.

He took a step forward, and when he did, a one-foot-by-one-foot square of the spongy earth pulled itself loose from the rest of the ground and hovered a few inches in the air, not too far ahead of him. Simon tilted his head with interest, visually inspecting this rubbery floating square, and then it began to spin, slowly at first, ramping up to a blindingly fast twirl within seconds. As the square tile spun, it changed color, brightening to a vivid emerald green. The square slowed, then it stopped spinning altogether, and Simon saw that it was no longer a square of rubber, but a square foot of grass.

It dropped back into the square hole in the ground, a perfectly geometric stamp of summertime grass amid a sea of spongy black material.

Simon hesitated. He looked around, to confirm that he was alone.

He stepped forward, planting one foot, then the other foot onto the grass.

As soon as he was standing on the grass, the rest of the ground broke into squares, and they all lifted into the air as one. Some went higher than others, but none of them was more than a few feet off the ground. They hovered for moment, then they, too, began to spin.

As they whirled at their dizzying pace, they turned green, became squares of grass, and lowered back onto the ground. Now the entire expanse was a long, bright meadow of brilliant green grass.

Simon smiled down at the field spread out before him. He'd never seen anything so beautiful.

Movement caught his eye, and he turned his head.

The grayish-blue cyclone was spinning right next to him.

Simon screamed in surprise and fell down backward onto the grass. The cyclone spun closer, and Simon threw up his arms to protect himself from getting sucked into its vortex. But magic wouldn't come to his hands. More than that, he didn't feel like he was getting sucked toward the cyclone; it was just spinning, and the spinning was having no physical effect on Simon.

Then the cyclone bent forward, as if leaning down to inspect the fallen human. Simon lowered his hands and looked up expectantly at the broad, spinning top of the small tornado.

Light is the maker and the master of shadow, said the cyclone.

"I remember," Simon said.

Oh. You do? the cyclone asked.

"Yes," Simon replied. "You said that before."

Oh, the cyclone said. It straightened up again, spinning in place for a few long moments. *I thought maybe you'd forgotten.*

"I didn't," Simon insisted.

Oh, the cyclone said again. *Okay, then.* The cyclone began to spin away, moving off toward the horizon.

"Goodbye," Simon called after it.

The cyclone stopped. *Oh. Goodbye,* it said. Then it continued on its way, and Simon watched it go.

"That was strange," Simon muttered when it had disappeared.

He got to his feet and took a step forward. When he did, the grass disappeared; the ground became the empty blackness of the universe, and Simon fell, and fell, and fell, screaming as he plunged into the darkness.

CHAPTER 23

"Simon!"

Virgil fell over his own feet as the man with the shaved head and with glowing blue palms leapt around the corner and slammed his hand into the side of Simon's head, shooting a concussive blue blast to his skull as he connected. Simon's head smashed sideways against the wall, and he crumpled to the floor, unconscious.

"Simon!" Virgil screamed again.

The man turned toward Virgil, holding up his hands in front of his chest, palms outward. A blue circle glowed in the center of each palm, as if light-up discs had been inserted beneath the skin. The lights grew brighter and brighter, and they began to hum with power.

Virgil's eyes grew wide as he realized what was about to happen. He raised his own hands and threw up two kinesthetic shields as the man with the shaved head shot two powerful brilliant streams of blue magic at Virgil's chest. The shots collided with the shields, and tiny orange bits flaked away as the attack began to cleave through the barrier. Virgil gritted his teeth and pushed more energy into his hands. Pulses of orange light flooded down his arms, and he threw all of his energy into the backs of the shields. They rocketed forward, slamming through the blue beams and smashing the man's hands against his own chest. The shields struck him so hard, there was a loud cracking sound as his bones popped under the impact.

The man howled in pain as he flew back against the wall and hit it hard enough to put a dent in the plaster. He sank to the floor. The magic drained from his hands, and the discs beneath his skin faded to a dull blue. He put one hand to his chest, gasping for the air that Virgil had knocked out of his lungs with his defensive attack.

Virgil approached the fallen man, his left fist glowing an angry red-orange. "The head shot was a huge mistake, Mortal Kombat," he snarled. He lifted his fist to strike, but just as he did, the man's eyes rolled up into his head, and he fell over, passed out from either fear of Virgil's power or from the excruciating pain of a shattered sternum.

Virgil chose to believe it was the former.

"Yeah, you'd *better* faint," he said.

He powered down his fist and ran over to where Simon lay in a heap in the hall. He knelt down and searched his friend for signs of life. He seemed to be breathing, though shallowly.

Virgil tapped him lightly on the cheek. "Simon? Are you alive?"

Simon's eyelids fluttered open. His eyes were glassy and unseeing as he came to. Then he blinked a few times, and his eyes began to focus on the world around him. "Shadows," he said.

Virgil frowned. "Shadows?" he asked.

"Shadows..." Simon replied, trailing off. He could just barely see a fading image of a dream he'd had, and the more he tried to focus in on it, the more completely it disappeared. "Something about...shadows..."

Virgil leaned over and inspected the side of Simon's head. "The good news is, there's no blood," he said.

"Yeah," Simon said, sounding confused. He looked around. "What happened?" He tried to sit up, but his head exploded with pain. He winced and groaned as he laid back down on the floor.

"The bad news is, you probably have *internal* bleeding. Or a concussion. Or a stroke. Is that what a stroke is?" Virgil frowned. "I've never known what a stroke is."

"I'm fine," Simon said, waving him away and sitting up more slowly. His head still hurt, but not as badly. "What happened?"

Virgil jerked a thumb across the hall. "Sub-Zero over there shot you with a magic blast at point-blank range."

Simon squinted at the unconscious man. "What happened to him?"

"I scared him literally to death," Virgil said proudly.

He reached down and helped Simon to his feet. Simon groaned at the pain, but once he was standing, the pounding in his head faded to a dull thud. "Do you think it's weird that suddenly *everyone* in Templar has magic powers?" he asked, trying out his balance and stepping gingerly across the hall.

"I still think it's weird that *we* have magic powers," Virgil admitted.

Simon crossed the hall and carefully approached the unconscious man. He charged up his right hand and holding it ready, in case the man woke up. With his left hand, he reached down, gripped one of the man's hands, and turned it over. "Look," he murmured.

Virgil trotted over and peered down at the man's palm. "Scars," he said, noticing the straight lines of raised scar tissue that ran near the heel of his hand.

"Surgical scars," Simon corrected him. He tapped a finger against the dull blue light in the man's palm.

The disc beneath his skin was as hard as stone.

"The Shadow Lord is having these people surgically enhanced," he said. "They're taking some sort of magical stones—or magical *somethings*—and they're surgically grafting them into non-magical people."

"Whoa," Virgil whispered, the enormity of that reality hitting him hard. "He's not just building an army; he's building a *magical* army."

Simon nodded. "Fifty bucks says this guy's name is on the list the Redditor sent us with a red X next to his name."

"Made younger by the Refracticore?"

"Yep."

Virgil shook his head slowly as a cold chill of dread crept through his chest. "We have to stop him," he said, his voice trembling just a little. "We have to stop the Shadow Lord."

Simon looked up at Virgil, his eyes both pleading and serious. "Virg," he said, his voice even, almost robotic, "look around you. Look where we are. Look what *they* are," he said, gesturing down at the magically-enhanced man on the floor. "It may already be too late to stop him." He stood up, putting a hand against the wall and steadying himself while his head pounded from the movement. "We need to figure out how big his army is," he said. Using the wall as a support, he shuffled down the hall.

"It doesn't seem like there are a whole lot of people here," Virgil pointed out. "We've seen, what, twenty or thirty?"

"There were more than thirty names on the retirement homes list," Simon reminded him. "It's a big house. Just because we haven't seen them yet doesn't mean they're not here somewhere. Or maybe they're just not here right now."

Virgil stopped in his tracks. "Maybe the shadow army is out in the world," he said. He shuddered at the thought.

"We have to figure out how big the army is," Simon repeated, his words sounding garbled, as if his tongue were too thick for his mouth.

Virgil gave him a sideways glance. "You hit your head *hard*," he said. "We should get out of here and find you a doctor."

But Simon shook his head, wincing with the pain. "Not yet," he replied. "Not until we figure out—"

His words cut out as he stepped into the next room. The plaque outside read GYMNASIUM, and the sprawling chamber certainly fit the bill; there was a basketball hoop at either end, and the shiny wooden floor had been marked over with tape that showed boundary, half-court, and three-point lines. But those tape marks were all but completely obscured by the scores of military-style bunk beds that lined the room, filling the entire space from end to end, and from side to side.

There were eight rows of bunks in all, and more in each row than Simon could count from his vantage point near the edge of the room. Each of the metal frames was wedged in so closely to the ones next to it that there was hardly room for a person to stand between beds.

The gymnasium had been converted into sleeping quarters for an army.

"There must be hundreds of them," Simon said in awe.

"And they each sleep two," Virgil added, his words hollow with fear.

"This can't be," Simon said quietly, stepping forward, into the maze of bunks. "There's too many…"

Something on the side the gymnasium caught Virgil's eye. He walked over and discovered a low bank of computer monitors set up on folding tables along the western wall. Each of the monitors showed a scene from a different security camera set up somewhere on the property. "Uh…Simon?"

Simon padded over to the monitors, using the metal rails of the bunk beds to keep himself upright. "What is it?"

Virgil didn't say a word. He just raised a trembling finger and pointed at one of the monitors.

It was linked to a camera that was mounted to the roof on the back side of the Grimsley house. The camera pointed down at the backyard; nearly the entire screen was filled with an image of Simon's giant sinkhole.

The guards standing at the top edge had lowered more ropes down into the pit, and now, they saw with growing horror, the people who had fallen into the sinkhole were climbing out.

Simon counted thirteen separate ropes leading down to the bottom of the hole. Every single one of them was covered by a swarm of people climbing up out of the pit. There were *dozens* of them, scrambling up the steep walls of earth and pulling themselves toward the top.

The Shadow Lord's soldiers must have been in the backyard when the sinkhole opened, Simon realized…training, exercising, running through drills—something. Nearly the entire army of the Shadow Lord had fallen into his sinkhole. Now they were climbing out, gathering in the yard above them.

And their numbers counted in the hundreds.

"We need to leave," Simon realized, his chest suddenly tightening with panic. "*Now.*"

Virgil threw his shoulder under Simon's arm and helped him out of the gymnasium and back along the hall. They climbed the stairs and wound their way back out of the house, slipping out the front door just as a series of angry shouts broke into the back of the house, signaling the return of the Shadow Lord's soldiers.

Simon and Virgil hobbled through the grass and across the boundary of mist, losing themselves in the swirling clouds and stumbling blindly through the Shadow Lord's fog.

CHAPTER 24

It had been a long time since Virgil had driven the Pontiac, but Simon was in no shape to sit behind the wheel. Virgil screeched onto the highway, nearly side-swiping an oncoming car that was barreling through the mist.

"Sorry!" Virgil called out as the other car screeched past them, blaring its horn.

"Careful," Simon muttered, closing his eyes and rubbing his temples.

"I'm plenty careful," Virgil insisted, careening around a curve. He looked over at the passenger seat. "Simon! Do *not* close your eyes!" He had seen enough medical dramas in his life to know that falling asleep while concussed was not something that was generally encouraged.

"I'm tired," Simon sighed, but he peeled open his eyes and tried to focus on the road.

"Just stick with me for another twenty minutes," Virgil said, speeding along the mountain road. "I'm taking you to the hospital."

"No," Simon said firmly. "Take me to Llewyn."

"Llewyn?" Virgil replied uneasily. "But Simon, we don't even know if Llewyn—"

"We're going to find out," Simon said firmly, cutting him off and leaving no room for argument.

Virgil sighed. "Okay," he said, pulling onto the interstate. "But *then* we're going to the hospital."

They pulled up next to the East River not long after, and Virgil hopped out of the car. Simon had a harder time of it; he felt sluggish, and his feet didn't respond as quickly as he wanted them to. But with Virgil's help, he managed to hobble inside the canvas tent, which was still lopsided from their quick reconstruction of it the previous week.

"We don't leave until we see Llewyn," Simon said.

"Okay," Virgil nodded.

They stepped carefully across the broken flagstone floor, making a wide arc around the splintered wood beams that used to be the staircases. "Where do we look?" Virgil asked, glancing around nervously. "Where do you think she—?"

Morgaine appeared before them in a puff of smoke, still dressed in her long-sleeve t-shirt and yoga pants, her wild brown hair now pulled back into a tight ponytail. She rested her hands on her hips and looked down distrustfully at the boys. "Looking for someone?" she asked.

"Llewyn," Simon croaked. "We want to fee Llewyn."

Morgaine squinted at him. "You want to *fee* Llewyn?"

"He hit his head," Virgil explained apologetically, "I think he has a concussion. We shouldn't even be here; we should be at a hospital."

"*Medicine*," Morgaine said with disgust, rolling her eyes. "One doesn't *practice* medicine, you know. One *learns* medicine, and one applies one's learning, but one doesn't *practice* it. There's not *art* in medicine!" She pushed up her sleeves and stepped forward, reaching out with both hands and touching her fingers against the sides of Simon's head, just behind his ears. "*Stille heede*," she said in a thick, Middle-English brogue.

The spinning sensation in Simon's brain melted away. The piercing whine in his ears disappeared. He gave his head a shake, and it didn't hurt.

"Huh," he said, rolling his head and knocking out the cobwebs. "Thanks."

"You're fixed, now you can go," she said, making shooing motions with her hands. "I have work to do."

"But Llewyn—" Virgil started.

"Llewyn is in no shape to receive visitors," she replied curtly. She lifted a finger and pointed to the door. "Go."

But Simon crossed his arms and stood his ground. "No," he said.

Morgaine looked taken aback. "I'm sorry? *No?*" she replied.

"We're not leaving until we see Llewyn."

Morgaine furrowed her brow. She crossed *her* arms, too, and for a few moments, they were facing each other down in a sullen standoff. "Is it me?" Morgaine finally said, breaking the silence. "You don't trust me? What do your histories say about me? Let me guess: Arthur was the hero, Merlin was the fool, and Morgan le Fay was the vile and treacherous snake."

"Close," Simon admitted, standing his ground. "Except for Merlin. He comes off as a powerful sorcerer."

"Except in the Disney version," Virgil pointed out. "He's kind of a bumbling idiot in that one."

Simon nodded. "I guess that's true," he said.

Morgaine threw her hands up in frustration, and she began to pace around the ruined living room in tight circles. "Unbelievable! And yet, so incredibly typical. The woman must be a shrew, a harpy! The men—oh, they write *songs* about the men, but gods forbid there be a woman with a little power, so they cast her as the witch." She turned back to the two young men, her eyes burning with anger. "You think I'm keeping you out because I've let Llewyn die? Puh!" She turned on her heels and marched down the broken hallway. "You want to see your wizard? Fine. Come with me. But don't say I didn't warn you when you're up all night with your terror-dreams."

She disappeared into the hallway, and Simon and Virgil exchanged a look.

"You said you wanted to see him," Virgil said. He gestured for Simon to go first.

They followed Morgaine through the labyrinth of halls, and they came to a stop outside a large, wooden double-door. The wood was old and weathered, with a series of wide metal bands crossing the planks, holding them together. Instead of knobs, the doors had heavy iron rings. Morgaine gripped one of the rings, then turned back to Simon and Virgil. "You were warned," was all she said.

Then she opened the door and let them into Llewyn's chamber.

There were no windows in the room, and the only illumination came from three floating balls of light that spun lazily near the ceiling, a good thirty feet above the floor. Simon stepped cautiously into the room, squinting into the darkness and trying to discern shapes from shadows. As soon as his foot touched the wooden floor, the three balls of light intensified just a bit, and they sank downward through the air. With each step, the light became brighter and brighter, and soon Simon could make out the sparse furnishings of the bedchamber: a modest wardrobe in the corner, a writing desk situated against the far wall, one small bedside table, and the bed itself, a simple wooden thing with stark pine posts and a thin, straw-filled mattress.

"Enjoy," Morgaine said, and she closed the door behind them.

Simon cautiously approached the bed. It was still too dark to make out the details of the vaguely-human shape lying on the mattress. He moved closer, and the lights lowered to just a few feet above the wizard. They threw their soft, orange glow across Llewyn's damaged form, and Simon gasped and recoiled in fear.

The creature lying in the bed was Llewyn Dughlasach, but it was a badly deformed version. The broken shards of him that had formed when he shattered on the ground had been gathered and arranged in more or less the proper order, but they hadn't knit back together into one smooth, whole person yet. Instead, Llewyn was made of small geometric chunks of person that had been properly positioned but not pushed all the way together. He looked like a complex, twisted Rubik's Cube of a man, or like a sculpture made of ice cubes.

"It's like someone glued melting Legos onto a skeleton," Virgil blenched, sidling up behind Simon and gaping down in horror.

"You'd not look better," the Llewyn-creature croaked. Virgil screamed and flailed backward, tripping over his own feet and landing hard on the floor.

Simon stared down in a sort of horrified wonder. "Llewyn?" he asked cautiously.

"I will be again soon," the wizard said. He didn't open his mislaid eye as he spoke, and his magical eye had gone dark. His jaw worked strangely, sliding to the side before it could move down to open his mouth, and as a consequence, his words came out sounding as rough and blocky as his body looked.

"We thought you were dead," Simon said, his voice quivering with emotion, and with relief.

"Not a bad alternative at this point," the wizard grunted.

"Does it hurt?" Virgil asked, climbing back up to his feet.

"Yes."

Virgil gave Simon a sideways glance. He nodded toward Llewyn, giving him a "Go on" motion. Simon grimaced, but he stepped forward.

"I know it's not a good time, and you're...healing," Simon said, searching for the right word. "But Virgil and I are in *way* over our heads with the shadow army, and we need help."

Now Llewyn did open his good eye. The eyelid had to slide to one side and then ratchet up to get around the protruding block that was currently his eyeball, and it did not look like an insignificant amount of trouble. "What shadow army?" he grunted.

Simon sighed loudly, and then he launched into the story of the last two weeks, starting with the Refracticore and the youth-draining elderly, taking him all the way through the discovery of the Grimsley mansion and the surgically-enhanced magical army. It was hard to know where to start, but once he got going, the words came easier and easier, until they were practically tripping over each other, racing off of his tongue. A couple of times, Virgil had to repeat something that Simon had garbled in his excitement, and when he finished with, "So now there's an army of hundreds, or maybe thousands, of magical warriors, and some of them don't have shadows, and we have no idea why," he gasped for breath, his lungs heaving against his ribcage.

Llewyn was silent for some time after that. Simon and Virgil looked down at him expectantly. The wizard slid his eyelid closed and seemed to settle into some sort of quiet stasis.

"Great...you broke him," Virgil mumbled.

But then the eye slid back open, and despite the strange, blocky nature of its surface, it looked more alert and cognizant than ever. "The Shadow Lord's power is growing. He must be stopped."

"Yeah," Virgil agreed sadly. "Templar is in serious trouble."

"Not just Templar," grunted the wizard. "And not just the world. Potentially the entire universe."

Simon furrowed his brow. "What do you mean?" he asked.

"Templar is a dimensional nexus," Llewyn said curtly, trying to measure his words. They could tell that it pained him physically to speak. His brain, his vocal cords, and all the connections between them were separated into chunks and haphazardly fused together; it must have taken an extraordinary will to close the loop and form coherent sentences. "Whoever controls Templar controls the gateway between our dimension and countless others. He who controls the gate will decide who—or what—comes through it. If the Shadow Lord gains control of Templar, the power over the dimensional gate will make him like a god."

"And some things that could come through the gate might have their sights set on our entire universe," Simon whispered carefully, finishing the thought.

"Yes," the wizard confirmed. "The Shadow Lord will test the psychic borders of the city, searching for the gate. His army will prod Templar for weaknesses. They will disturb creatures that have been long asleep. We should prepare for an influx of paranormal activity."

Virgil raised an eyebrow in concern. "*More* paranormal activity?" he said.

Llewyn grunted. "More. And if he finds the gate, his army will protect it. If they are the legion you describe, it will be almost impossible to cut them down when they are assembled in front of the gate. The Shadow Lord must be stopped. Now."

"Okay," Simon said slowly, his voice trembling. "But... how do we do that?"

Llewyn's misshapen body relaxed, and his eyelid slid closed once more. "I don't know," he said.

Simon and Virgil exchanged looks. *Not good,* Virgil mouthed. Simon shook his head in agreement.

Llewyn managed to lift one Lego-block hand and wave it slightly through the air. From somewhere outside of the room, they heard the heavy *clunk* of a lock sliding back in its chamber. "Take your manacles from the trunk," he said. "And whatever you do, do *not* ask Morgaine for help. Her magic comes with a heavy price."

Simon shifted uneasily. "Can we trust her?" he asked.

"No," was Llewyn's curt reply.

CHAPTER 25

"Hey, we have an email!"

"We have email?" Simon asked, blinking himself back to reality.

They had left Llewyn's chamber and, after stopping by the unlocked trunk in the front room to grab their manacles, they had found their way through the maze of the wizard's mansion to the new opening between the magical canvas tent and their office. They had been sitting in relative silence, thinking about Llewyn's words, and his warnings.

Or, at least, Simon had been thinking about Llewyn's words.

Virgil had been tapping around on the internet.

"Of course we have email," Virgil said, rolling his eyes. "It's not the sixteenth century. I set it up a couple days ago."

"But we don't even have a computer," Simon pointed out.

"Why do you act like such an old person sometimes?" Virgil groaned. "I'm the one with the gray hair." He tossed his phone to Simon.

Simon took the phone and looked down at the email. His eyebrows narrowed. He held the phone screen back up to Virgil. "It's a blank message," he said.

"Yes, Grandpa Simon, it is a blank message," Virgil replied, rolling his eyes. "It's from Templario."

Simon winced. "How did Templario know our email address?"

"Because I told him. On Reddit. Look, I don't have all day to explain the wonders of the internet, Simon. Just open the attachments."

"There are attachments?" Simon asked, confused.

Virgil grumbled something under his breath and snatched back his phone. There were six PDFs attached to the email, and

Virgil pulled them up with a few quick taps. He scrutinized the documents, then shook his head and handed the phone back to Simon. "I give up," he said, "what am I looking at?"

Simon turned the phone onto its side and zoomed in on the first PDF. "It's some sort of chart," he said. "From SouthPenn Energy."

Virgil winkled his nose. "Templario sent us his electric bill?"

"No..." Simon said, trailing off as he swiped around on the chart. "This is incredible," he mumbled. "Each page is from a different SouthPenn bill, but they're not Templario's. They're for the City of Templar."

"Why did he send us the city's utility bills?" Virgil asked.

"I don't know," Simon admitted. "But look at this..." He showed Virgil one of the pages, which was a bar graph with five separate bars. The original bars may have been in color, but the scanned PDF was a photocopy, and all five bars were various shades of gray. Four of the bars showed as extremely small, barely even registering on the graph. But one of them—the second from the left—towered over them like a skyscraper, reaching up to the top of the chart and dwarfing the other four bars. "These pages are all charts showing the electricity usage for all five of Templar's subway lines. Look at this...I mean, subways use a *lot* of power, right? But those four barely even show up on the chart compared to this one."

"So one of the lines is using too much power?"

"It's using *way* more than too much power. This is an astronomical level," Simon said, frowning down at the chart and chewing thoughtfully on his bottom lip. "Like, Refracticore beam-level."

"Which line is it?" Virgil asked.

Simon looked up at him and arched one eyebrow. "Guess."

Virgil grunted. "The orange line."

"Bingo."

"Man." Virgil pushed himself away from his desk and began to pace around the newly-refurbished office. "The shadow-servant disappears down there during a blackout, it's sucking down all the electricity, it suddenly attracts new riders like Peter Grimsley the Twenty-Eighth...what is going on with the orange line?"

Simon swiped through the collection of PDFs, analyzing each of them in turn. "Whatever it is, it's only been going on for the past four months," he said. "The records from five and six months ago show all five trains operating at energy levels that are more or less even." Simon tossed the phone back to Virgil, and he sat down in his chair, lost deeply in thought as he swiveled from side to side. Finally, he sighed, shook his head, and said, "I think we need to go check it out."

"Check what out?"

"The orange line."

"You want to ride the subway *again*?"

Simon shook his head. "I don't mean we should check out the train. I mean the tracks. Something's happening down in that tunnel that's using an insane amount of power, and it's tied to the Shadow Lord. We have to go find it."

Virgil stopped pacing. "Okay..." he said slowly, his mind racing. "But...go find *what?* What are we even looking for?"

"I don't know," Simon admitted. "Something that's sucking down power."

"You want us to just go on a jaunt along electrified subway tracks?"

"I know it's dangerous," Simon sighed.

"And illegal," Virgil pointed out.

"And illegal," Simon agreed. "But you heard Llewyn. The Shadow Lord has to be stopped. He has to be stopped *now*, before he finds the dimensional gateway. Our only other lead is Grimsley Manor, so unless you want to go take on a few hundred surgically-enhanced magical soldiers who are probably still pretty mad about falling into a sinkhole we made—"

"*You* made," Virgil corrected him quickly.

"—then we need to do this. Because we have to do *something*."

Virgil nodded, exhaling loudly. "Templar needs heroes," he said.

"Maybe now more than ever," Simon replied. His phone buzzed, and he fished it out of his pocket. A text from Abby popped up on the screen: *Sorry just got off work. Heading home to work on Insta ads. Unless u need me? Virgil ok?*

Simon glanced up at his friend. Virgil was stubbing his sneakers at the new hardwood floor, making screeching noises. As Simon watched, Virgil kicked down and hit the ground so hard that he tripped over his own foot and almost went careening into the fireplace.

Simon smiled.

Same old Virgil.

Yeah, false alarm, he typed back. *He's just the normal 'found a mansion full of evil shadow soldiers who don't have shadows' kind of not ok. You know.*

"What's the best time to go breaking and entering on electrified city property?" Virgil called out from across the room, picking himself up from the floor.

"The orange line runs twenty-four hours, so the later the better. It'll be less crowded. Let's go at midnight."

"That's, like, four hours past Grandpa Simon's bedtime, but okay," Virgil said with a grin. "What are we going to do, start at one end and work our way down until we see something that's electrically supercharged? Because there's, like, a million miles of track."

"Well, first of all, it's more like twenty miles of track," Simon said, smiling and shaking his head. "And second of all, we're not walking end-to-end. I have a feeling I know where to start."

CHAPTER 26

"Nobody panic: I got Snack Packs."

Virgil lifted the pudding cups out of the grocery bag and plopped them into Simon's purple Jansport backpack.

"You were supposed to be getting supplies," Simon pointed out with a frown, adding a few bottles of water to the bag.

"Snack Packs *are* supplies," Virgil insisted. "We could be down there for hours. We could get lost and be down there for *weeks!* We should have food, just in case."

"We're not going to get lost; we're following a set of train tracks," Simon said, rubbing his temples. "They run through, like, twenty stations, all of which have exits we can go through. And I'm not sure pudding is exactly survival food."

"It's food for the survival of my spirit," Virgil replied.

Simon sighed. "What else did you get?"

"Two flashlights…a nylon rope…dark ski masks…" Virgil said, transferring each item from the grocery bag to the backpack as he ran down the list. "I'm pretty sure the guy at Save For Days thinks I'm going to rob a bank."

It was just after ten o'clock, and they were sitting in their cramped apartment living room, huddled over the cheap Ikea coffee table with the backpack between them.

Simon checked his watch. "It's only ten," he said, stifling a yawn. "I don't know if I'm going to make it to midnight."

"I'm shocked," Virgil said sarcastically. He zipped up the backpack. "Well…do you think the subway is dead enough at this time of night?"

"Maybe don't use the word 'dead,'" Simon said uneasily. "But yeah, I checked the schedule. The orange line goes into late-night mode at 9:30 on weeknights."

"All right," Virgil said, clapping his hands and standing up. "Then let's go commit a super-dangerous felony."

"Got your manacle?" Simon asked.

Virgil pulled up his sleeve to show the light gray cuff on his wrist. "Reunited, and it feels so good," he grinned.

They locked up the apartment and hit the sidewalk. Virgil headed toward the Pontiac with the backpack slung over one shoulder, but Simon didn't follow him. Instead, he turned and walked toward the end of the block.

"Hey! Where are you going?" Virgil asked, jogging after him.

"To the orange line," Simon said, confused.

"On *foot?*"

"Yeah."

"But that's, like, two miles away!" Virgil whined.

"I know, but we don't know where we're going to end up. I'm not taking the 6000 out just to leave it by a subway stop that might be halfway across town from where we end up. Besides, if we move the car now, we'll lose our parking spot. We *never* get a spot right in front of the building."

Virgil groaned. "Can't we take a Lyft?"

"Do you want to pay for it?"

"I spent all of my money on pudding cups and ski masks," Virgil frowned.

"Then I guess we're walking."

They trudged along to the nearest orange line stop, a thirty-minute walk that took them through the cobblestone streets of Old Templar and up toward the Juniata River. The night was dark and quiet; Old Templar was primarily a commercial district, and it wasn't a great scene for nightlife, especially in the middle of the week. The moon was hidden by a thick layer of clouds, and the cold wind that blew through the darkness was a constant reminder that winter was on the horizon.

They eventually made it to the Mabel Street station. Above ground, it was little more than a dirty metal railing around a set of stairs that led down beneath the sidewalk. A rusty sign with cracked and peeling paint marked it as MABEL STREET, and a sickly orange light sat atop the sign, signifying the train line below.

"You're right...the subway's depressing," Virgil said as they crossed the street and stepped carefully down the stairs.

The station was empty, except for the transit employee sitting in her metal booth near the turnstiles. Her attention was focused on a book in her hands, and she didn't even look up as Simon and Virgil approached the entrance. They swiped their cards and pushed their way through the turnstiles, entering the dimly lit tunnel that led out to the underground platform.

"So what's the plan?" Virgil whispered, although there wasn't another living soul in sight. "Put the masks on now?"

"Yeah, put the ski mask on so the attendant can watch you do it on the security cameras, because she definitely won't think that's terrifying and immediately call the cops," Simon replied.

"Hmpf," Virgil muttered. "I'm picking up some sarcasm, and I don't think I like it."

"You're not the only one who can give it," Simon said proudly. He punched Virgil gently on the shoulder. "I think we should wait here for the next train to come. They're scheduled every fifteen minutes at this time of night, so that gives us some time. Once the train passes, we climb down and head north." He pulled the backpack off of Virgil's shoulders, set it on the floor, unzipped it, and pulled out the flashlights. "Here," he said, handing one up to Virgil.

"What about the ski masks?" Virgil asked.

"We can put them on in the tunnel. We just have them so that if a train does come, hopefully the conductor won't see us.

If he does, there's a pretty safe bet we'll be sitting in a jail cell when Templar falls to the Shadow Lord."

"I guess we *do* give off a pearly white glow," Virgil said, frowning down at his hands. "Geez. I should get some more sun."

"We'll take a vacation when we've saved the world," Simon said, zipping up the backpack and throwing it onto his shoulders. He nodded down the tunnel. "Here it comes."

The train rumbled slowly through the tunnel, squealing against the metal of the tracks. Simon and Virgil stepped back from the platform edge, huddling behind a concrete pillar as the train slid into the station. The doors opened, and a few passengers got off.

The conductor poked her head out the window of the front car, looking back down the side of the train to help gauge when to close the doors. But no one was getting on the train.

She looked over at Simon and Virgil. "You two riding?" she asked.

"Uh...we'll get the next one," Virgil said.

The driver shrugged and pulled her head back inside. But then she poked it back out. "What's wrong with this one?" she asked.

Simon and Virgil looked at each other, both of their brains scrambling to come up with a response. "Too...fast," Simon finally blurted.

The conductor gave them a bewildered look. Then she shrugged a second time. "Suit yourself," she said. She pulled her head back into the car and got the train moving again. It rumbled slowly down the tracks, disappearing into the tunnel.

"Too fast, huh?" Virgil said with a snicker.

"Shut up, I panicked," Simon mumbled. "Come on, let's go."

He approached the edge of the platform and peered down at the tracks. "The last rail is the one that's electrified," he said. "If you touch it, you're dead."

"No need to sugarcoat it," Virgil said. He pushed past Simon and was starting to lower himself over the edge when Simon grabbed him and pulled him back.

"Wait!" Simon hissed.

"What?"

Simon nodded toward the ceiling. Virgil looked up and saw a security camera above their heads.

"You think she's watching?" Virgil asked.

"I think even if she's not, they'll have a record of us going in, and that can't possibly be good."

"Hmm. Yeah. Good point." Virgil lifted his sleeve, revealing the gleam of his manacle. "Should I blast it to smithereens?"

"No, Bugs Bunny, you shouldn't. A broken camera will draw even more attention," Simon pointed out.

"Then what do we do?"

Simon pressed his lips into a line, thinking carefully. "I have an idea," he said.

He sent a stream of kinesthetic energy into his fist. He turned his hand over and opened his fingers. A soft ball of light sat in the center of his palm. He lifted it gently into the air, and it floated up lazily toward the camera. As it rose, the ball pulled apart, splitting into two separate balls, and then each of *those* split into two *more* balls, until there were four distinct light orbs floating up through the air.

They spread out from each other as they rose, moving along the center of the platform. Virgil chuckled with admiration as he realized what was happening: the four balls were positioning themselves beneath the four security cameras in the station.

Once they were all in place, the orbs rose more quickly, slithering up through the air and getting closer and closer to the cameras. "Get ready," Simon said out of the side of his mouth, concentrating on directing all four bits of magic at once.

They floated up until they reached the lenses of the cameras. Then Simon flared open his hand, and all four balls of light burst into bright flashes. While the lights burned so brilliantly, Simon knew, the computer monitors would show nothing but glaring white screens.

"Go!"

They jumped down onto the tracks. Simon hit the inner rail at a bad angle and stumbled, pitching forward toward the electrified third rail. Virgil reached out and snatched him back, hauling him to safety by the back of his jacket.

"Thanks," Simon muttered.

"I'm a real hero," Virgil replied.

They dashed into the tunnel just as the floating light orbs faded away, clearing the view for the security cameras.

For just a split second, the screens showed the dark shadow-figures of two young men slipping down the tracks and into the darkness.

CHAPTER 27

Simon knew it would be dark in the tunnels beneath the earth.

But he didn't fully realize what that darkness would mean.

The train tracks curved north after leading out of the station, and after just a couple of minutes of walking, the lights from the Mabel Street station were cut off by the tunnel walls, plunging Simon and Virgil into a darkness so total, so complete, it felt like an actual physical presence that pushed in on them from every angle. Their flashlights helped alleviate the darkness, of course, but they also served to make it more oppressive; the narrow beams of light made the expanse of darkness around them even blacker by comparison.

"I don't like it down here," Simon mumbled.

"You can't see it because it's dark, but I'm making a very surprised face right now," Virgil said sarcastically.

They hugged the left side of the tracks, giving the electrified rail a wide berth. They could hear the gentle humming of electricity coursing through the metal, and it made the hair on the back of Simon's neck stand up.

"Remind me what we're looking for?" Virgil asked.

"Something that requires an insane amount of power," Simon replied. He swept the flashlight over the walls and saw nothing that struck him as out of the ordinary—just curved cement walls streaked with dripping water and mildew.

"The air feels wet," Virgil complained. "I'd better not catch asthma."

"You can't 'catch' asthma," Simon pointed out.

"Then I'd better not get moldy lungs."

"No promises there. We must be getting close to the Juniata River. The tunnel eventually runs right underneath it; the air will get wetter the closer we get."

Virgil shivered. "You know I'm not claustrophobic, but the thought of walking through a tunnel beneath the Juniata…it gives me the creeps."

"Me too," Simon said. "But if I'm right, I don't think we'll need to go quite as far as the river."

"Why not?" Virgil asked, blenching as he stepped over the withering carcass of a dead rat.

"Because I'm guessing we only need to go as far as the spot where the shadow-servant vanished off the train."

Virgil scratched the top of his head through the ski mask, which they both wore rolled up over their brows. Dressed all in black and wearing the masks like caps, they looked like henchmen from the old Adam West *Batman* television show. "Good, 'cause this thing is getting itchy."

Simon pulled out his phone and checked the time. "We only have a few minutes until the next scheduled train," he said. "We'd better move."

They continued around the bend, pushing on through the darkness, which somehow seemed to get even more total as they progressed. Simon tilted his flashlight upward, and he saw that the dark gray concrete of the ceiling had given away to a strange matte black, as if someone had painted the tunnel. He moved the light down over the walls, and there was no mistaking it: the tunnel itself was getting darker.

"Guess that's either a really good sign, or a really bad one," Virgil said, seeming to reading Simon's thoughts.

"I guess it's both," Simon replied. "I think it means we're getting close."

They moved around the bend, and the flashlight beams illuminated the space ahead where the tight tunnel opened up to the wider chamber, where their train had lost power earlier that morning.

It felt like days had passed since then.

A drop of water plunked down on Simon's shoulder, and he screwed up his face in disgust. He wasn't a germophobe, but the idea of the filth the water must be picking up between the ground above and the subway tracks below made him feel a little nauseous.

"Is it raining down here?" Virgil asked, putting out his hand and catching drops on his palm.

"We must be even closer to the river than I thought," Simon murmured. But that didn't make sense. They hadn't even reached the Juniata River station yet, and that station, he knew, was on the south side of the river. They still had at least a few hundred yards before they reached the riverbed. Even if the tunnel structure were severely cracked—and it almost certainly *was* severely cracked—that much water shouldn't have been dripping through.

"It's weird," Simon said, holding one hand up to shield his head from the drops, which were getting worse with every step. "It's almost like—"

He tilted the flashlight up toward the ceiling once again, and his words choked off before they could leave his throat.

"Almost like what?" Virgil prodded. He raised his eyes to follow the arc of Simon's flashlight beam. "Oh," he whispered.

"Yeah," Simon replied. "Almost like the ceiling *itself* is dripping."

And that was exactly what was happening.

The thick black coating was collecting at a thousand different points high above their heads and dripping down its liquid darkness like rain. It was like standing beneath a freshly painted ceiling that had been slathered with way too much paint.

"What *is* that?" Virgil asked, disgusted, as he crossed his arms over his head, trying to keep the drops out of his mouth.

"I don't know," Simon answered. "But I feel like I've seen this before…"

"You've seen a subway tunnel dripping liquid death before?" Virgil asked sourly, pushing past Simon and hurrying toward the chamber. "Ugh. It smells like licorice and sulfur."

"I *have* seen this before," Simon insisted quietly, speaking more to himself than to Virgil and trying to jar the memory loose. "Where have I seen it?"

"Probably in your nightmares. It's like some sort of demonic liquid candy," Virgil replied, hustling out into the open space of the chamber. "Aw, man, it's even worse in here," he whined.

"Demonic," Simon said, brightening. "*That's* where we've seen it! On the flowers outside of Mrs. Grunberg's house! When we fought Asag, this was coating the flowers!"

"Oh yeah," Virgil said slowly, remembering. "The flowers were black, and they dripped shadows."

"And we thought it was because of Asag."

"The internet confirmed that," Virgil reminded him.

"The internet was wrong. It wasn't Asag that made the flowers black; it was the Shadow Lord. He was in that house with Neil. It's not *demons* that make shadow-liquids…it's *shadows*."

Virgil snorted. "Well, when you say it like that, it sounds kind of obvious."

Simon focused his flashlight on the drops coming down from the ceiling, and sure enough, they were smoky-black droplets that evaporated with a soft *pfffth* as soon as they hit the ground.

"The Shadow Lord must be close," Simon said, his voice as hard as stone. He rolled up his jacket sleeve and focused energy on his manacle, setting the dark gray cuff glowing with a vibrant orange. "Be ready," he advised Virgil.

"Got it," Virgil replied. He pushed up his sleeves, too, and set his own manacle glowing. "*Man* it feels good to have this baby back," he grinned.

Simon stepped out into the wider chamber, flashing his light around to get a feel for the space. It looked much as he remembered it, with wide walls and a high ceiling. Now that he had an unobstructed view of the entire chamber rather than just one side of it, he could see that there were actually six different archways set into the walls; three of them fanned out on either side of the main track, each leading to another dark tunnel that branched off in a different direction. All six of the portals had train tracks that split off from the main track and curled toward the archway; all but one of those tracks had been broken apart just a few feet from the main line, made useless for the train and blocked by the metal barricades Simon had noticed earlier. A person could walk into the tunnels, but a train car couldn't push through into the depths.

But there was one archway that still had its sidetracks still intact. The opening of that archway was blanketed by a thick darkness, like a veil of oil.

"This place weirds me out," Virgil said, trembling from a shiver that rippled through his shoulders.

Then a furious wolf-creature leapt out at them from the shadows, howling with rage and mauling Simon to the ground.

CHAPTER 28

"Simon!" Virgil screamed.

He was so shocked by the sudden attack that he dropped his flashlight. It clattered to the ground, bouncing off the metal rails and throwing its light across the room. In the flash of the beam, he saw a lightning-fast mass of fur streak across the chamber, disappearing into one of the tunnels, leaving Simon heaving on the ground.

"Simon!" he shouted again, sprinting over to where his friend lay sprawled across the concrete floor.

Simon kept his eyes squeezed shut. "Did it bite me?!" he asked in a panic. "I can't look— did it bite me?!"

Virgil picked up Simon's flashlight and shined it over him. "I don't think so," he said. He pulled back the collar of Simon's shirt and jacket, checking his shoulders for puncture wounds. He sat back, exhaling a deep breath. "You're lucky he didn't take your arm off."

Simon lifted his left hand into the air. His manacle glowed a sickly orange color. "I blasted him," he said weakly.

They heard a snarl from the tunnel behind them, and Virgil grabbed Simon under his arms, pulling him to his feet. "Not hard enough," he said. "He's coming back for more."

They tensed and pointed themselves toward the dark, gaping maw of the tunnel, both of them firing up their manacles. Virgil's fingers twitched with anticipation, and sparks popped from his fingertips. The snarling got closer and closer...and then the wolf appeared, leaping through the opening and hitting the ground for one step before launching back into the air and lunging at Virgil, teeth-first. Virgil cried out and shot a blast at the wolf's throat that went wide and singed the animal's arm instead. With his other hand, Virgil threw up a shield just in time, and the creature smashed into him, taking him down to the ground.

They had fallen into the path of the flashlight beam, and Simon got a decent look at the creature. It was a wolf, without a doubt, but it also had the powerful arms and broad shoulders of a man, and Simon knew he was looking at his first real-life werewolf.

Simon powered up his hand and aimed his palm at the werewolf, but the creature and Virgil were too close. "I can't get a shot!" he yelled. "Get him clear!"

"*You* get him clear!" Virgil cried from beneath the monster's snarling, slavering jaws. He was holding his shield with two hands now, and the wolf was pressing the shield down on him. If it didn't snap in half, it would slowly crush the air from his lungs.

Virgil twisted on the ground and got first one foot, then the other up underneath the shield. He let go with his hands and threw them onto the ground for support. Then, groaning from the strain, he pushed against the shield as hard as he could with his legs. He kicked up, and the werewolf and shield flew backward. It was only a few feet, but it was enough for Simon. He blasted a powerful stream of energy that caught the werewolf right in the chest.

The creature went down, hitting the ground like a sack of bricks.

Simon sidestepped carefully over to Virgil and reached down with one hand. "You okay?" he asked.

"Yeah," Virgil nodded, taking Simon's hand and climbing to his feet. "That really wasn't too—*watch out!*" He knocked Simon out of the way as the werewolf picked itself back up, shook its head, and sprang again. Simon spun to the side, but not quickly enough. The werewolf swiped down with its razor-sharp claws, and though it didn't take out the chunk of Simon's chest that it was aiming for, it did slice into his shoulder, drawing shallow channels of blood through his skin.

Simon grunted in pain and tumbled to the ground, rolling onto the tracks. He looked to his left and saw the glow of train headlights heading toward them from around the bend in the tunnel. "Train!" he called out, trying to ignore the pain in his shoulder.

"Little busy!" Virgil called back. He had reached into his psychic vault and retrieved Gladys. He launched the wooden ball forward, and it connected with the werewolf's injured arm with a loud, sickening *crack*. The werewolf howled, a sound that reverberated through the subway chamber and shook loose even more of the shadow droplets.

Gladys zoomed back into Virgil's hand, and he fired her a second time, but this time the werewolf was ready. He struck out with one big paw and knocked Gladys to the ground. She pinged off the railroad track and shot across the chamber, rolling to a stop near the mouth of one of the abandoned tunnels. Virgil reached out and called for her, but Gladys seemed dazed and was sluggish in responding.

The werewolf stalked around to the side, nursing its wounded elbow. Thick strings of spittle dripped from its snout, and its eyes flashed dangerously in the darkness. Virgil took a shot at the beast with his manacle, but the werewolf ducked it easily.

Simon rolled over and started to push himself up from the ground when something caught his eye, just outside of the flashlight beam. It was the small, thin shoot of a weed that had pushed its way up through the concrete floor of the subway tunnel. He snatched up the flashlight and shined it around the space. The floor was covered with the small, determined stems.

"Simon! A little help?" Virgil cried. The werewolf pounced at Virgil, and he threw up a barrier with his left hand and charged up his manacle with his right. The werewolf smashed into the orange shield, but this time, Virgil managed to stay on his feet. He reached around the shield with his right hand and fired a magic blast at the creature. It caught him in the belly, but it only seemed to make the werewolf angrier. It picked up a chunk of concrete rubble from the ground and hurled it at Virgil. He caught it with the shield, but the force of the impact knocked him backward across the chamber, stumbling over the railroad tracks and just barely missing the electrified third rail.

"Working on it!" Simon replied. He shot a blast at the werewolf to lay down some cover for himself, then he charged up his left hand and held the kinesthetic magic in his fist until it glowed like fire.

It was time to take a page out of Virgil's book, or else break every single bone in his hand trying.

He leapt up into the air and swung down hard with his fist on the descent, screaming with fear and determination as he slammed his hand against the concrete beneath him. To his extraordinary relief, the cement cracked and shattered under the force of his magic, and he blasted a hole through it that reached down to the earth below.

The werewolf lunged at Simon, but before it made contact, a dark blur steaked across Simon's vision, and Gladys clocked the creature right in the side of the head. The werewolf crumpled and fell to the ground in a heap, dazed and struggling to get its bearings.

"Thanks," Simon murmured.

"Don't mention it," Virgil replied.

The headlights from the subway were barreling around the corner. "Watch the train," Simon said.

"Thanks for the pro tip," Virgil said, rolling his eyes. He pulled his ski mask down over his head, and Simon did the same, although it occurred to both of them that while the dark head-to-toe outfits might conceal them from the conductor, odds were that the massive, snarling half-human monster was going to be a little obvious. "They're going to see the werewolf," Virgil pointed out.

"Working on it," Simon said again. He charged up his hand, filling it with deep ochre-colored energy, and he placed it into the hole he'd punched through the concrete. He dug his fingers into the earth below. The magic flowed out of his hand and into the cold, hard dirt. Simon closed his eyes and willed the magic to spread beneath the ground, to seek out the weeds. The green shoot in front of him soaked in a stream of the kinesthetic power, and it began to grow, slowly at first, yawning upward, then picking up speed, expanding in circumference, too, pushing up from the ground in a long, waving stalk.

The magic spread through the ground and found other weeds, and soon the entire chamber was filled with a small forest of writhing green plants pushing up through the cracks in the cement.

Simon opened his eyes. The werewolf was shaking its head and stumbling up to its hind legs. Simon narrowed his eyes at the creature and whispered, "Now."

In unison, the weeds snapped forward, reaching out like whips, wrapping around the werewolf's arms, his legs, and his torso. One weed shot forward and tied off the werewolf's snout, cinching it shut. The werewolf reared his head back and roared, snapping the weed with his powerful jaws, but then several other tendrils shot forward, winding around the creature's muzzle and snapping it closed. The werewolf struggled against the bonds, but more and more weeds flicked out, encircling the monster until nearly his entire body was covered in green coils.

The werewolf thrashed madly, but the more he pulled, the tighter his bonds became. Then the weeds began to contract, dragging the creature back across the concrete floor.

"Whatever you're doing, do it faster," Virgil urged, hopping anxiously from one foot to the other. He glanced nervously down the subway tunnel. The train was getting closer.

Simon threw more force behind his will, and the weeds pulled harder, yanking the furious werewolf through the air. The animal managed to snap one arm free, and it sliced down with its claws, tearing at the weeds that bound its snout. It had sliced through half of them and was about to struggle free of the weeds' grip when the stalks dragged him down across the third train rail. There was a loud zap, and the werewolf stiffened as currents of electricity shot through its body. It went limp then, and though its chest still heaved against the weeds, the monster was unconscious.

The weeds lurched over to one of the abandoned tunnels and released the werewolf in midair, sending its huge, heavy bulk spinning down into the darkness of the tunnel.

Simon yanked his hand out of the dirt, and the weeds snapped back down to their regular size. Simon grabbed the flashlights and flicked them off, and he and Virgil dove back against the protection of the stone wall just as the train rolled out of the close tunnel and into the larger chamber. They caught a glimpse of the driver's face as he stared out the front of the window, blinking hard and looking confused. The driver pressed a button, and the train picked up a bit of speed, and Simon exhaled with relief; the driver was less interested in figuring out what he had just seen and much more interested in leaving whatever it was far behind.

They watched as the train's taillights disappeared into the next tunnel, leaving them alone in the darkness.

"Think he saw the werewolf?" Virgil asked once the rumble of the train had died away.

"I'm pretty sure he at *least* saw the flashlight beams," Simon replied.

"Think he'll call it in?"

Simon shrugged. "Guess we'd better be quick, just in case."

"Yeah." Virgil glanced uneasily at the tunnel down which Simon had thrown the werewolf. "What about him?" he asked, pointing at the darkness. "He's going to wake up eventually."

Simon nodded. He powered up his manacle and aimed it at the top of the tunnel opening. He fired a powerful blast that shattered the concrete, and giant chunks of cement crashed down into the tunnel, blocking the way out. "That should hold him long enough."

"Long enough for what?" Virgil asked.

Simon turned and faced the dark, glistening black wall that covered the only other tunnel with train tracks running into it. "That's where the shadow-servant went when he disappeared from the train. I'm sure of it."

Virgil stepped up next to Simon, staring at the tunnel, with its thick, glossy curtain. The blackness shimmered just a little, like there were tiny ripples spreading through the surface. "Do you think that's the gateway?" he asked quietly. "The one Llewyn was talking about?"

Simon frowned, and he shook his head. "Llewyn said the Shadow Lord would use his entire army to protect the gateway between dimensions. He'd have sent more than just one shadow-servant. I don't think it's the gateway…but I *do* think it's a portal." He took a step closer, and he shined the flashlight at the opening to the tunnel. Whatever was covering the opening, it completely absorbed the light, swallowing it whole.

Virgil bit his bottom lip nervously. "A portal to *where?*" he asked.

Simon took a deep breath, and he exhaled, letting the air pass slowly out of his lungs. He turned to Virgil and said, "I think we found the Shadow Realm."

CHAPTER 29

Abby rubbed her eyes and stretched. She checked her watch. It was getting close to midnight.

She picked up her phone and looked at the screen. Still no word from Simon.

"You'd better not be dead," she mumbled. She set down the phone and turned back to her computer.

She had never made a digital ad before, and it had taken her most of the night. She'd sprung for some cloud-based design software and figured she'd make Dark Matter Investigations reimburse her when they finally got some revenue flowing. The first two hours of her night had been filled with tutorial videos, which she found frustrating and not nearly as helpful as they were meant to be. It had taken her another half of an hour to get the picture of Simon and Virgil adjusted so it wasn't too dark, and once she'd done that, she began the long spiral down the rabbit hole of figuring out how to get an ad on Instagram.

She was really starting to hate technology.

But finally, at long last, she had completed a draft of the Dark Matter ad, and although her eyes were burning from spending almost four straight hours staring at her laptop screen, she forced herself to click the ad preview so she could give it one final check before she sent it live to the people of Templar.

She clicked open the preview.

The image popped up, and she banged her head down on her desk.

"Come. On. You. Stupid. Thing!" she hissed, knocking her head against the wood with each word. She picked herself up and stared down at the disappointing preview image. Even after all of her tweaks, the photo was still too dark. It looked amateurish.

She would have to take another picture tomorrow and start all over.

If Simon and Virgil both came back from the subway tunnels alive.

She pictured Simon's flattened body smooshed against the front car of the orange line, and she was a little bit consoled by the fact that if he got hit by a train, she wouldn't have to keep working on this stupid ad.

Abby let out a heavy sigh and pushed her hair back out of her eyes. As her hand passed in front of her vision, she noticed the black speckles on her palm for the hundredth time that day. Morilan's mark. She figured it would probably stay with her always.

Eh, she thought, tracing a finger over the dots, *it actually looks kind of cool.*

She decided to give up on the ad for the night. She was reaching up to close the laptop when she suddenly remembered the other photo she'd taken of Simon and Virgil that morning, the first photo, when her flash had been on. The image was probably too washed out from the brightness of the flash, but it definitely wouldn't be too dark. It was worth a look, at least, in the very, *very* slim chance that she could manipulate it into something useful.

She picked her phone up again and flipped through her photos. She found the picture and zoomed in. Her face wrinkled up in disappointment when she saw it up close. The picture was definitely too washed out to be any good.

Abby was about to set her phone back down when something else about the photo caught her eye. She brought the screen closer and looked carefully at the image. Her pulse began to race, and she could feel the hot blood pumping through her eardrums as she scanned the photo.

"No," she whispered, her voice hoarse from the fearful tightening in her throat. "No, no, no!"

Her entire body flushed with panic as she closed out the photo album and tapped open her text messages. She scrolled back to the earlier texts from Simon and read his words again, carefully:

He's just the normal 'found a mansion full of evil shadow soldiers who don't have shadows' kind of not ok.

Abby's stomach turned, and she felt the tingling sensation of standing on the edge of a skyscraper roof, looking down. She opened the photo album again and pulled up the washed-out image of Simon and Virgil.

The room had been so dark, and the flash had been so bright. Simon and Virgil had been standing in front of a wall. In the photo, both of them were wincing, looking away from the glaring light of her phone. On the wall behind Simon was his shadow, huge and looming and dark.

And on the wall behind Virgil, there was nothing.

It was just a blank, white wall.

Virgil didn't cast a shadow.

Her veins turned to ice as another one of Simon's texts flashed across her memory:

Something's up with Virgil. Something's wrong.

"Shadow soldiers who don't have shadows," she whispered.

Something snapped in her brain, and she flew into action. She dialed Simon and held the phone up to her ear. It went straight to voicemail.

"Come on, *come on!*" she hissed, trying again. But the phone didn't even ring. Simon, she realized, wouldn't be getting much service in the tunnel.

She opened up her messages and typed, *DON'T TRUST VIRGIL!!!*

She hit send and prayed that the text would go through.
Then she typed it and sent it again, four more times in a row.

CHAPTER 30

"Should we go through it?" Virgil asked, approaching the subway tunnel with the inky black veil. He reached out a finger, as if to poke the shimmering surface.

Simon raced up and slapped his hand down. "Don't *touch* it!" he cried, grabbing Virgil by the arm and dragging him back. "You don't know what it does!"

"I'm guessing it separates the Shadow Realm from our world," Virgil said sharply, indignant at being slapped away. "We came here to fight the Shadow Lord, right? Let's go see if he's home."

"You want to just march right through a dimensional portal and face a powerful shadow-wizard in his own home?" Simon snapped back, just as sharply.

"That's what we came here for!" Virgil cried, throwing his hands up in frustration. "That's exactly why you brought us down here! What are we even *doing* here if we're not going to follow through?!"

"I'm not saying we're not going to follow through! I'm just saying, let's think about it for a second." Simon pressed his hands to his temples. "And the point of being down here isn't necessarily to fight the Shadow Lord. We came down to figure out why there's so much electricity being used." He crouched down and inspected the train tracks. The rails that disappeared into the Shadow Realm branched off the main tracks, but they could connect if the controller threw a switch. Even with the rails disconnected, a set of power cables were fastened to the third rail of this side track into the Shadow Realm, giving it juice. "I think the tracks are pumping power through the portal to keep it open," Simon decided.

Virgil grunted softly. "I hate to admit it, but I've seen enough movies that I think you might be onto something," he murmured, looking down at the tracks.

"Which means we don't *have* to go through the portal and face the Shadow Lord."

Virgil frowned. "We don't?"

"No," Simon said, his mouth set in a hard line of resolve. "All we have to do is cut the power. Once the portal closes, the Shadow Lord will be trapped in the Shadow Realm."

Virgil stiffened. His mouth turned down in a worried frown. "Well...but what if he's not *in* the Shadow Realm? What if he's on this side?"

"Then we'll at least cut him off from his seat of power," Simon said. He stepped between the railroad tracks, positioning himself above the cable that connected to the third rail and fed it electricity. "Disconnecting the cable should do it."

"Wait!" Virgil blurted out, reaching forward and grabbing Simon's arm. "Are you insane?! You'll electrocute yourself!"

Simon pulled his arm away, shrugging out of Virgil's grasp. "The cable's wrapped in a rubber sheath," he pointed out. "And my shoes have rubber soles. I'm just going to stomp down on it. I should be fine."

But Virgil shook his head. "There's enough electricity running through that thing to fry an entire city!" he cried.

"Then I'll just blast it."

"No! You don't know what that might do!" Virgil shrieked. "Let's go get a—I don't know, a *real* tool, something *made* to smash through an electric current. We'll come back later and take care of it when it's safe!"

"Or we can take care of it now and put an end to the Shadow Lord!" Simon felt his phone buzzing in his pocket. Whoever it was had terrible timing. He ignored it.

"It's not safe!" Virgil insisted. He grabbed Simon again, dragging him back from the cable.

Simon had to lurch forward to wrench himself out of Virgil's grasp. "Let go of me!" Simon shouted.

"Let's go through the portal and finish off the Shadow Lord, like we said we would do!" Vigil yelled back, his voice tight.

"We never said we would do that!" Simon yelled. His pocket vibrated again. His fingers clenched as he bit back the irritating itch of the phone against his hip. "I'm cutting the power, and we're ending it!"

"We can't!" Virgil cried. "We have to go through the portal!"

"*Why?!*" Simon exploded. His phone buzzed *again*, and he fought back the urge to snatch it out of his pocket and throw it against the concrete wall of the chamber. Suddenly, all the confusion and distrust and anger that had been seeping into Simon's bones over the last twenty-four hours began to bubble up inside his blood. "You have been acting *so* weird!" he shouted. "You lashed out about Abby for freeing Morgaine, you've been totally spaced out all day, you're saying things that aren't *you*... what is wrong with you?!"

"Nothing's wrong with me!" Virgil fired back. "You say we're going to take down the Shadow Lord, but when you get a chance to do it, a *real chance* to do it, you back off! We could have started something at Grimsley Manor, but you said, 'No, let's run away!'"

"We would have been slaughtered if we'd tried to take on the army at Grimsley Manor!" Simon hollered.

"And now we're down here," Virgil shouted back, ignoring Simon's protestations, "we are within *striking distance* of the Shadow Lord himself, and you want to run away!"

"I don't want to run away; I want to smash the connection to the portal so the whole gateway collapses!" Simon shouted, gripping the flashlight so hard that the plastic casing squeaked. He was screaming, and his voice was echoing off the close walls of the chamber, reverberating in his own ears in a way that set his teeth on edge. "Why are you so stupidly insistent on sending us into the Shadow Realm?"

His pocket vibrated again, and Simon screamed, unleashing a torrent of indiscernible curse words as he ripped the phone out of his pocket. "*What?*" he yelled at the phone, looking down at the screen.

He had four missed text message from Abby. They all said the same thing.

Simon felt his throat go dry as the moisture evaporated from his tongue. His own fingers felt alien to him, as if they belonged to someone else, and he was just borrowing them to hold the phone while his eyes searched for meaning in the words splashed across the screen.

DON'T TRUST VIRGIL!!!

Simon felt numbness prickle across his skin. He raised his phone and showed Virgil the screen.

"What is this?" Simon asked, his voice high and strange in his own ears.

Virgil leaned in and read the words that Abby had sent. He read them, and his whole demeanor changed. His shoulders relaxed, and his frantic eyes softened into a look that was calmer, more subdued. Watching the transformation was like watching a snake shed its skin.

"Aw, Simon," Virgil said. His voice sounded cold and distant, almost like it was someone else talking through a speaker hidden in Virgil's throat. He looked at his friend with empty eyes, and the corners of his lips turned up into a calculating smile. "You weren't supposed to find out yet."

Then he reached out and gave Simon a hard shove, pushing him back through the gateway, and Simon fell screaming into the dark world of the Shadow Realm.

CHAPTER 31

Simon fell hard onto his back, and the wind burst out of his lungs, leaving him breathless on the cold, hard ground of the Shadow Realm.

His mind spun in frantic circles. *Abby's text. Virgil's betrayal. The Shadow Lord's reach.*

And his own despair.

Simon rolled over onto his stomach. He drew in short, gasping breaths. The air felt heavy in his lungs. The space around him was filled with a strange light. He struggled to his knees. This world felt familiar, but completely alien at the same time. There was grass beneath him, well-tended and closely cut, dark emerald in color, the blades perfectly still in the unmoving air. He sank his fingers into the grass, desperate for a feeling of familiarity in the new dimension.

It helped, but only a little.

As his breath came back to him, Simon's eyes cleared, and his brain began to register the landscape of the Shadow Realm. The light was colored a rich burnt orange, fueled by the simmering sun that hovered low in the sky before him. Simon turned his head and found that he was in a courtyard, surrounded on two sides by high, dark hedges that stretched up toward the sky, creating imposing and insurmountable walls. Behind him, the hedges closed in and framed a tall, dark gateway lodged in the middle of the wall, the Shadow Realm's side of the passage. And in front, sprawling out to either side, was a huge, tar-black castle, its sharp, jagged turrets stabbing upward into the burnt-orange sky.

Virgil hadn't just shoved Simon into the Shadow Realm. He had forced him into the trap that was the Shadow Lord's front yard.

The enormity and the danger of his situation settled onto Simon's shoulders like a heavy weight. He was in a strange dimension, in the stronghold of the evil Shadow Lord, betrayed by his best friend for reasons his brain couldn't even begin to comprehend.

The alien sun burned in the sky like a campfire marshmallow that had caught on fire, with huge tongues of flame rolling up the sides of the sphere and licking toward the sky. The strangeness and the intensity of the sun threw long shadows across the realm, so that the dark green grass was made mostly black by the shadow of the broad, angular castle and the high, blocky hedges. The shadows themselves had a different density here than they did in Simon's world. They were thick, so instead of walking *through* a shadow, a person would walk *into* one, almost like they were fording a shallow creek.

Simon shivered. A voice inside his head told him to turn and run back through the portal.

But he was way ahead of the voice.

He scrambled to his feet and rushed back toward the gateway, slipping on the grass. He lurched forward toward the inky black veil, but he felt something tug at his right arm. He looked down and recoiled in fear at what he saw: a piece of the hedgerow's shadow had reached up, taken on actual dimensions, become completely solid, and grabbed him above the elbow with a claw made of solid, black smoke-like shadow.

Simon spun around and tried to yank his arm free, but the shadow was strong, and it held tight, digging its sharp fingers even deeper into his skin. Simon sent a kinesthetic blast into his fist, but when he did, he didn't feel the familiar warmth of the flowing magic. He looked down at his hand. It was just an empty hand, with no trace of magic to be seen.

"What the...?" he breathed, wrinkling his brow in confusion.

A voice broke across the yard, then, or maybe it was just in Simon's own head; he couldn't tell...it was deep and booming, and it reverberated his skull:

You have no magic in this place.

"The Shadow Lord," Simon whispered.

The dark puppet master who had been pulling the strings of Neal Grunberg, of the woman in the purple cloak, of the elderly traitors, of the shadow army—he was there, in the Shadow Realm, watching Simon from his castle stronghold.

Not just watching, the voice of the Shadow Lord said, reading his thoughts. *Waiting.*

It was a confirmation of what Simon already knew: Virgil was working for the Shadow Lord now, and had escorted him to the gateway for the purpose of sacrificing him to the darkness.

"Let me go," Simon said, trying to sound even and brave, but the words came out like a whimper.

I have no plans to keep you here, Simon Dark. I need you in Templar, putting your extraordinary powers to work on my behalf.

"I would never work for you," Simon whispered, straining against the shadow claw. Another hand formed from the hedgerow shadow and snatched up Simon's other arm, and together, the two claws dragged Simon forward across the lawn, his shoes sliding easily over the dark, wet grass.

Virgil said the same. You see how little he meant it.

Simon seethed with anger, pulling back at the hands that gripped him and dragged him forward, toward the Shadow Lord's castle. "What did you do to him?" he demanded, hissing the words through gritted teeth.

No, came the Shadow Lord's response. *I wouldn't want to spoil the surprise.*

The shadows pulled Simon into the center of the courtyard, and the sharp towers of the dark castle rose over him ominously, blocking out the flaming orange sun. In the center tower, a large, shuttered window opened from the inside; a matching window was open on the back side of the tower, so that Simon could see a huge rectangle of dark orange sky through the center of the tower. A beam of burning sunlight shot through the new opening, framing Simon in a box of light amid the shadows on the courtyard grass.

The hands of shadow that gripped his wrists spun him hard, and he slipped around on the wet grass so that he was facing away from the castle, looking down at his own shadow, which stretched across the yard, dark and abnormally long in the low-angled light. The hands caught his wrists again, and two new shadow-claws snatched out at him from the darkness beneath the hedgerows, each one grabbing an ankle so that he was held tightly by all four appendages. Simon cried out in alarm and frustration, and he kicked his legs. But the shadows were strong, and they lifted him into the air, suspended at four corners above his own shadow.

"Let me go!" Simon screamed, flailing against his bonds. But it was no use. He was helpless against the strength of the Shadow Lord.

As he struggled, his shadow writhing beneath him, another dark shape emerged from beneath the hedges. It was a long, thin blade, black as onyx and sharp as the steel of a Japanese sword. Simon stopped thrashing and stared in horror down at the black blade, which extended toward him from the shadows. The sharp edge of it gleamed in the orange light...it seemed to hum as it moved through the air.

Simon's breath caught in his throat as the blade came closer. "What is that?" he asked, his voice cracking with fear.

But the Shadow Lord remained silent.

The blade slid forward, and the claws around Simon's ankles gripped even tighter, holding him immovable in the air.

The blade rose until the flat side rested just against the tip of Simon's right shoe, with the sharp end pointing toward his heel, back toward the castle.

Then slowly, the blade began to slice along his foot.

The dark sword only ran along the outside of his shoe, but Simon could feel the sharpness of the blade as if it were slicing through his skin too, and he screamed. It was as if the blade was sawing through a long piece of his flesh, stripping it from the nerve tissue and muscle beneath. Tears streamed down his cheeks as Simon's screams echoed through the realm, disappearing through the hedgerows, evaporating into the uncaring world beyond the courtyard.

The sword finished its slow, painful slice, and Simon's right foot burned with an intense, raw fire. He gasped for breath, his chest heaving between his cries, and he looked down at the ground before him.

His shadow was still stretched out across the lawn, but now, the part of the shadow that had been cast by Simon's right leg dangled freely on the grass, as if it was flexing its knee, testing out movement, even though Simon's leg was still held tight by the shadow-claws.

The blade had separated Simon's shadow from his foot.

A second dark sword reached out from the other side of the courtyard, a mirror image of the first, and began the long, cruel process of slicing through the space beneath Simon's left shoe.

The pain was excruciating.

The sword made slow, careful progress, and when it had passed all the way to the heel of the shoe, Simon dangled in the air, his feet flaming with pain, and his shadow spun away on the grass, freed from the moorings of Simon's body.

This is what happens, Simon thought dully, his mind numb with pain. *This is how the surgeons at Grimsley Manor lost their shadows.*

They too had gone through this torturous process.

And so had Virgil.

The shadow claws released him, and Simon fell to the ground, landing hard on his feet. He screamed as shockwaves of hot pain jolted through his legs, and he collapsed, sucking in air through clenched teeth and biting back the tears in his eyes.

But the shadows weren't done with him yet.

His own shadow, now freed, did something extraordinary: it pushed up from the ground, gaining dimension as it did, filling out like a swelling balloon and taking the shape of a human. As it peeled up from the grass, its dark features became more and more defined, until it stood proudly on its own two feet, a perfect shadow sculpture of Simon Dark.

Simon gasped at the transformation, a cold terror washing over his body. The shadow Simon stepped forward with a wicked grin on his face, and Simon pushed back on his hands, trying to scramble away. But the grass was slick, and his feet were in such pain that he didn't cover much ground. His living shadow came upon him easily, stepping over him, planting his feet on either side of Simon's ribs, straddling him and grinning down, his dark eyes glistening with evil intent. The shadow crouched down until he was sitting on Simon's chest; Simon convulsed against the ice-cold feel of his shadow-self that radiated from the creature's skin. Shadow Simon reached down with his solid black hands and gripped Simon's mouth, sticking its fingers inside and pulling at his lips, pulling his mouth open so wide that his jaw stretched and popped.

Then the shadow Simon began to change. A tendril sprouted from the top of his head, twisting in the air like a tentacle. It reached downward and slid into Simon's mouth, and Simon watched with horror as the shadow-creature's head began to shrink, all of its mass squeezing into the tendril, making it longer, and with a terror he had never thought possible, Simon realized what was happening.

His shadow was entering his body, where it would take total control.

The tendril snaked its way into his throat, and the process of turning Simon into a subservient shadow-creature began.

CHAPTER 32

Simon fought to retain control over his own mind.

His brain wanted to shut off, to block out the trauma, to send him to another place, to make bearable the fact that his body was being infiltrated by his own evil shadow.

But Simon fought for clarity.

He couldn't give up. Not yet.

As he faded in and out of consciousness, his vision wavered between the orange-black sky of the Shadow Realm and the bright neon-light streaks of color in the dark-sky place from his dreams. His subconscious was trying to pull him down into a dream, and fighting to stay awake was exhausting.

"Stop," he heard himself say, his voice reverberating through the dark-sky place. "I need to fight my shadow."

I know...duh, said a familiar voice. Simon turned his head and saw the grayish-blue cyclone hovering just to his right. *That's what I've been telling you.*

Simon crinkled his brow in confusion. "What?"

The cyclone let out a heavy sigh.

Light is the maker and the master of shadow. I've said it, like, five times now.

"Light is the maker and the master of shadow?" Simon repeated, bewildered.

Yeah. You know. Lights makes shadows. But it also controls them.

Simon thought about this. He felt like his brain had been covered in glue and stuck to a wall, and he was slowly trying to peel it loose. "I can control my shadow...with light?" he asked.

Again, said the cyclone, *duh.*

Simon squinted, working hard to get his thoughts to make sense. "But I don't...have my magic," he said slowly. His tongue felt thick in his own mouth, and it was hard to make the words come out.

Well, that is a problem, the cyclone agreed. *I can't help you there.*

"How do I—?" he began, but the cyclone interrupted.

Whoops, you're almost past the point of no return. You'd better get back.

The small, grey-blue tornado rushed forward, slamming into Simon with its swirling winds, and when Simon opened his eyes again, he was back in the Shadow Realm.

Shadow Simon had formed himself entirely into a long, serpentine rope of shadow now, which was feeding itself down Simon's throat. Simon choked and gagged, his eyes stinging with tears as they searched the space frantically. He could stop the shadow if he could control the light, but the only light came from the sun, which was completely out of Simon's control.

But then he looked up at his hand, and he was shocked by what he saw there.

He had forgotten about the flashlight he'd been holding when Virgil pushed him through the gateway.

It was still in his hand.

With a clumsy thumb, Simon pushed the switch, and a gentle beam burst out from the lens. He swung it around in a wide arc, and the light sliced through the shadow tentacle.

Simon rolled over onto his stomach and gagged, tugging at the severed tendril that was halfway down his throat. He pulled it back up, coughing and choking, and flung the dark, mucous-covered rope into the hedges.

He sputtered for air, his face red and burning, his lungs heaving.

As he worked to catch his breath, the shadow claws snapped out again, snatching at his wrists. Simon spun quickly, waving the flashlight like a light saber, cutting through the thick darkness with his light. He scrambled to his feet, gripping the flashlight with both hands and backing slowly away toward the portal.

Stop him! the voice of the Shadow Lord screamed.

More shadow arms slapped out from the darkness, and Simon spun in a frantic circle, blasting through the shadows, cutting them all down as they stretched across the courtyard. He moved toward the gateway, but stopped when he looked down at his feet and saw that he had almost reached the edge of the rectangle of light that shone down through the opening in the castle. The shadow beyond the edge of light seemed to quiver in anticipation; he knew if stepped into that darkness, the shadows would consume him.

He pointed the flashlight down at the castle's shadow, burning a wide hole in the darkness. He could sprint forward keeping himself in the light if he kept the flashlight pointing downward...but then he would be defenseless against the shadows snapping out from the edges of the yard. As if reading his mind, another claw shot forward, and Simon just barely swung the flashlight around in enough time to chop through it.

In addition to everything else, he saw movement from the hedges as the slithering tail of his shadow-self wriggled free from the greenery and rolled across the ground. It reunited with the rest of his deformed shadow, molding itself back into the shape of Simon.

"Come on," he whispered to himself, gritting his teeth. "Think, think, think."

Then the shutters in the castle window began to close, and his rectangle of safety collapsed in on itself.

The answer came to Simon like a bolt of lightning, and just in time. He snatched his phone out of his pocket and flicked on the flashlight, holding it out in front of him while he pointed the stronger flashlight beam down at his feet. The shutters slammed closed, plunging the courtyard into shadow, but the flashlight kept him in a circle of light. Even his own legs didn't cast a shadow anymore; their shadow had been sliced away, too. It allowed for a full circle of protection around him. He was grateful for that much, at least.

The castle shadows swirled with anger, globs of concentrated darkness circling around him like sharks. Another hand shot out from beneath the hedges, and Simon moved his phone, catching it in the light. The shadow evaporated. But the phone light wasn't as strong as the flashlight beam, and the claw was allowed to get a little closer than Simon would have liked before it dissolved in the glow.

It was time to move.

His feet were still burning, and every step was agony, but Simon forced himself to run. He kept the flashlight pointed down at his feet as he tore across the grass, waving the phone light around his head, shining it in every direction like he was swatting at flies. The shadows reached out, and a few of them even grazed his arm and scratched his hip, but he was quick with the phone light, and he cut through them all in the end.

He was just a dozen yards from the gateway when Shadow Simon stepped in his path.

Simon gritted his teeth and pushed forward. The claws had fallen away, and his shadow-self was the only thing standing between him and the real world. He swung his arm around and shone the phone light at Shadow Simon, pointing it at his chest. A hole melted through the dark sternum, but Shadow Simon still stood. Simon moved the light around, cutting through the shadow in a zig-zag pattern, and Shadow Simon shifted as new openings cut through him. As Simon moved the phone, Shadow Simon closed up the dark spaces behind the roving circle of light so quickly that Simon couldn't cut his shadow-self down; every time he swiped the light through his torso, Shadow Simon filled in fast enough to keep himself on his feet.

As small as his phone light was, the trick wouldn't work on any shadow creatures more than a few inches wide.

Simon cursed under his breath.

If he couldn't cut the shadow creature down, he would have to go through it.

Simon charged forward on his pained and burning feet, each step sending shockwaves of agony up his legs. Shadow Simon reached his hands forward; his arms stretched, becoming longer and thinner, moving toward Simon like snakes. Simon clamped his mouth shut and dove forward, slicing up through one arm with his phone light. The other arm gripped him by the neck, but Simon swung the light around and cut through that arm, too. Shadow Simon pulled his hands back into himself, reforming like a Play-Doh doll, but Simon lunged beneath his arms, barreling forward, shoulder-first. He lifted the flashlight beam at the last second, burning a wide, gaping hole through Shadow Simon's midsection. Simon turned the wrist that held the phone and tilted the light downward, evaporating the newly-reformed shadows beneath his feet that stretched up to snare his ankles, then lurched forward, smashing through the hole in Shadow Simon, his shoulders bursting through the shadow-creature's waist and tearing him in half. Simon felt the chill of the shadow's cold as he shot through it, and the top half of the Shadow Simon fell to the ground, completely severed from the lower half.

Shadow Simon pulled himself together and reemerged from the darkness, an evil look of frustration on his face…but Simon had hit the ground running, and the last thing he heard before he dove through the portal back to the real world was the furious howling of the Shadow Lord in his ears.

CHAPTER 33

Simon hit the ground hard, slamming his shoulder onto the concrete and skidding across the solid metal rail of the train track.

His feet burned; his shoulders were shaking with cold. His lungs hurt, his throat was raw, and he was exhausted.

He opened his eyes and saw Virgil standing over him, examining him with curiosity.

"How did it go?" Virgil asked.

Simon's eyes blazed with anger. "What did you do with Virgil?" he seethed.

"Oh," Virgil said, his face falling into a frown. "So it didn't go great, then." He tilted his head in confusion. "How did you manage to get away?" he asked, genuinely curious.

Simon pushed himself up to his feet, facing Virgil with his legs tensed and his hands balled into fists at his side. "What did you do with Virgil?!" he demanded again.

Virgil raised his hands defensively. "I *am* Virgil, Simon! Look at me." He gestured to himself. "I *am* Virgil!"

"You're a shadow that's controlling Virgil," Simon corrected him. His jaw clenched so tightly that it squeaked.

Virgil shrugged and spread his hands wide, as if to present himself. "I know. I'm the whole package," he grinned.

Simon welled up with such intense anger that both hands began to glow orange from the magic he didn't even realize he was sending into his fists.

"Whoa, whoa, whoa!" Virgil cried, shrinking back and ducking behind his own arms. "Shadow on the inside, but Virgil on the outside! Blast me, and you blast Virgil first!"

Simon's hands shook with rage. "Let him go," he said, his voice quivering.

"Well, I can't really do that, because it's not part of the plan. Plus, while I'm in here, I'm holding all the cards," Virgil said, scratching the side of his head. "But, counteroffer! How about you just go back into the Shadow Realm, let your shadow inside, and then you and Virgil can help take over Templar together? It could be like a friend activity! A real bonding experience," he beamed.

Simon lifted his left hand and pointed it at Virgil. Small flecks of light began to swirl in front of his palm as the powerful magic gathered inside of him.

"Hey, come on, no joke," Virgil said seriously, taking another step back, "if you kill me, you kill your best—"

Simon didn't wait for him to finish. He lowered his hand, pointed it at the power cable that fed into the train track that led into the Shadow Realm, and fired a blast that exploded the cable, severing the connection. The metal rail lost power, and the portal evaporated, dissolving from the center outward until the last bits of silken black sheen disappeared around the edges of the tunnel.

"*No!*" Virgil screamed. He ran forward, blowing past Simon and sprinting into the tunnel. He passed right through the opening and kept going deeper into the train tunnel, with the cold metal tracks disappearing into the darkness before him.

The portal to the Shadow Realm was gone.

"What did you do?!" Virgil screamed. He reemerged from the dark tunnel, pulling at his hair with both hands. His face was red and swollen with anger. "You have no idea what you've done!"

"I trapped your master in his own world," Simon shot back.

"*Trapped* him? You haven't *trapped* him!" Virgil shrieked, his voice pinging off the concrete walls. "It's like throwing a blanket over a raging bull. You haven't *stopped* him; you've only slowed him down, and made him angrier! Who do you think he's going to take that out on?!" He raised his right hand. His manacle glowed dangerously, and he fired a shot at Simon's chest.

Simon threw up a shield and caught the attack easily, so Virgil fired a second, and a third. Simon knocked them all away, but the attacks were forcing him backward, and he couldn't watch where he was going. When Virgil fired the next blast, Simon tripped over the track rail and fell hard onto his back. His head whipped backward, and he caught it, just inches from the electrified third rail. Virgil picked up a chunk of broken concrete from the floor and hurled it at Simon's head. Simon reacted just in time, twisting to the right as the concrete struck the rail. It bounced off the metal and scraped against his ear, drawing three thin lines of blood against his skin.

"Ow!" he cried. He pushed himself up carefully, avoiding the electrified rail, and clapped a hand to his injured ear.

Virgil paced furiously, like a wild animal who had been caught and caged. "You think this saves you?" he seethed, flexing his fingers and stomping across the floor. "You think this *saves* you?!" He picked up the busted end of the cable, his hand protected by the rubber sheath, and shook the frayed, sparking end at Simon. "This is nothing! This is *nothing!*" He threw the cable back down. "Do you know what he'll do to me for letting you close the door? Do you know what he'll do to *Virgil?!*" There was real terror in his voice, and in his eyes. "You *don't* know, Simon! You don't know what he does when he's disappointed! You don't know what he did to Neil!"

That caught Simon off guard. "Neil Grunberg?" he asked. "He drove Neil insane and got him sent to prison."

"Neil's not in prison! Not anymore," Virgil sneered. "Don't you watch the news? It's the only thing on in our stupid office!"

He kicked the curved concrete wall of the chamber and grunted from the pain that shot through his toes. "Neil *disappeared* from prison. Vanished. Gone."

"Gone?" Simon asked. "Gone where?"

"That's the part you won't hear on the news. Neil was dragged into the shadows." He pointed toward the tunnel that until recently had led to the Shadow Realm. "Neil's in there. He's in the dungeon of the castle, because he failed the Shadow Lord. Do you have any idea what happens to people in the Shadow Lord's dungeon?"

Simon shook his head slowly. He didn't know...but he could guess at just how bad it might be.

Virgil shuddered at the very thought of it. "That's what happens when you fail him. You being here, and closing the door, that means *I* failed him. You know what he'll do to me when he gets back?" Virgil shrieked. "You know what he'll do to *Virgil?!*" He closed his fist, and it glowed bright orange with power. "I'm sorry, Simon. I really wanted this to work. If you'd have just given in...we would have been unstoppable. But you ruined it. I have to make it right." He raised his arm, which glowed violently orange in the darkness of the chamber. "The only thing now is to kill you." He fired a powerful kinesthetic stream at Simon.

Simon held up a shield, and it caught the blast, but the stream of magic kept coming, and it was stronger than any Simon had seen from Virgil before. It was as if the shadow inside of him had made him stronger and was focusing all of its fear and anger on the kinesthetic attack. He used both hands to hold the shield before him as the power of Virgil's fury pushed him backward. His shield began to splinter; Simon didn't know how much longer it would hold. He raised his free hand to fire a shot back at Virgil, but his shield hand wasn't strong enough to hold off the attack by itself. He had to drop his other hand back down to support it. He couldn't attack, and he couldn't keep holding the power back.

Simon looked around desperately for help. He took two steps to his left, drawing Virgil's magic over to the side of the chamber. He stepped behind a chunk of concrete; just as his shield began to crack in half, he dug his toes beneath the cement brick and kicked it up at Virgil's chest. Virgil ducked out of the way of the flying missile, breaking his magic stream and giving Simon a chance to drop his shield and power up his manacle. Virgil recovered and resumed his attack, blasting a wide stream of orange energy out through his palm. But Simon returned fire, shooting his own kinesthetic blaze back across the tracks, and the two streams of power smashed together, battling back against one another in a bright, hot explosion of magic. Virgil's attack gained some ground, then Simon's pushed back harder, moving toward Virgil. Back and forth, the advantage alternated.

Simon began to drip with sweat from the strain of firing his magic, but Virgil, fueled by rage, had a seemingly endless supply of emotion, and he wasn't tiring. Slowly, his attack was winning out over Simon's, pushing its way closer and closer to Simon's hand. If it reached his palm, the magic would burn through him.

Simon had no illusions about the fact that Virgil, controlled by the shadow, would actually kill him.

He kicked up another piece of rubble, but this time Virgil was ready, and he raised his free hand and blasted it out of the air without breaking the kinesthetic stream from his palm.

Simon was breathing heavily now, and his arm had grown weary from forcing back against Virgil's magic. He lifted his right hand and conjured the weeds up through the cracks, and he sent them to attack Virgil, but between his battle in the Shadow Realm and his fight against Virgil now, he was so tired, and his hand wasn't making its direct connection with the soil. The weeds had little magic to draw from, so they traveled lazily toward Virgil's feet, and he kicked them away easily.

Simon fell to his knees, barely holding his magic together. Sensing his weakness, Virgil moved closer, stepping over the tracks and bearing down on Simon with a sneer. When he was within arm's reach, he closed his hand, and the magic blast stopped. With nothing left to push back against, Simon cut off his magic, too, and collapsed down onto his hands, gasping for breath. His hair hung down in wet tendrils; his shirt was soaked through with sweat.

He looked up at Virgil, panting. "Virgil," he wheezed, "I know you're in th—"

Before he could finish, Virgil powered up his left fist and slammed it into Simon's jaw, punching him hard with a kinesthetic blast. Blossoms of red burst in front of Simon's eyes as his jaw exploded with pain. The force of Virgil's blow knocked him over, and the side of his head skidded against the concrete as he slid across the floor.

"Virgil..." he said weakly, looking up at the shadow that wore his friend's body.

His vision swayed in and out of focus as Virgil stepped over to him with murder shining in his eyes. He charged up his fist again and slammed it down at Simon's head. Simon threw up a weak shield, and Virgil smashed straight through it, grazing the crown of Simon's head with the punch. He pulled back and fired again, and this time, Simon didn't have the strength to even try protecting himself. Virgil's power-punch connected with him at the temple, hitting him so hard that he blinked out of consciousness for a few seconds.

When he came to, he was lying on his stomach, sprawled out on the ground.

His feet were raw and screaming from the removal of his shadow. His arms were weak from the strain of fighting Virgil's magic. His breath was shallow; his ears rang. His head throbbed, his mouth bled, and his jaw ached. His whole body felt sapped and empty.

Simon had nothing left to give.

The tunnel that led from the Mabel Street station began to glow. A train appeared, charging quickly down the tracks.

The light cut through the darkness in Simon's vision like a lighthouse lamp through fog. The train was coming. If he could only buy himself some time...

Simon pushed himself to his knees like a punch-drunk boxer. Virgil stepped up and kicked at his ribs. Simon squirmed away, but he wasn't fast enough, and Virgil's foot caught him right in the side. It wasn't hard enough to break any bones, but it took away what little air was in Simon's lungs. He rolled over onto his back, wheezing and staring up at the ceiling. His eyes glassed over with exhaustion, and he lolled his head helplessly toward Virgil. Simon moved his lips, but they had trouble making the sounds that they were supposed to make. He licked his lips and tried again, but still, the words came out as less than a whisper.

"What?" Virgil asked, holding up a hand to his ear in a mocking gesture. He grinned and squatted next to Simon's shoulders as the train moved closer. "You've got to speak up."

Simon tried again, but his lungs couldn't push enough air through his vocal cords to make the words loud enough to hear.

Virgil sighed with frustration, and he lowered his ear to just above Simon's mouth. "What?" he said again.

Simon cleared the blood from his mouth. His voice was a wet rasp as he said, "I'm going to save you." Then he jammed his head upward, connecting his skull with the side of Virgil's head with a loud, sickening *crack*.

Virgil cried out and stumbled backward, falling onto his seat and clapping a hand to his head. The train barreled out of the tunnel and through the open chamber. With his last bit of strength, Simon opened both of his hands, and tiny balls of orange light lifted up from them, floating up into the air. They flattened out into threads as the train rushed past, and they wrapped around Simon's wrists while their other ends flew out and coiled around the metal railing that crossed the last car of the train. Then the threads contracted, and Simon was lifted off the ground, pulled through the air after the rushing subway, secured by his glowing orange threads.

The magic threads reeled themselves in, pulling the barely-conscious Simon onto the relative safety of the hard metal platform of the car. Then they repositioned themselves, lashing him to the railing, securing him tightly to the back of the train as it plunged into the next tunnel on the far side of the chamber, heading toward the next station and leaving a stunned and furious Virgil behind.

CHAPTER 34

"Whoa. Simon. You look *awful*."

Abby slid into the café booth, her brow furrowed with concern. She reached across the table and took Simon's hand in her own. Simon winced; his palm was raw from the sheer amount of magic he'd pushed through it in his battle against Virgil, but he bit back the pain and let her hold his hand.

It felt nice to feel her touch, even through the cotton of her glove.

"I feel..." he began, but his jaw had begun to swell where Virgil power-punched him, and talking was more painful than he expected. He grimaced and tried again: "I feel pretty awful."

The waitress came over and dropped off two coffees. She glanced down at them suspiciously, taking note of Simon's bruises before moving away.

Abby lowered her voice to a gentle whisper, unsure how to ask her next question. "Did Virgil do this to you?"

Simon closed his eyes and exhaled. "He's...not himself right now."

"So it's true, then? He's part of the Shadow Lord's army?"

Simon nodded grimly. He began to explain, but Abby could tell that the effort of speaking too much was causing him discomfort, so she shushed him and pulled off one of her gloves. She laid her hand gently down on Simon's arm and let his emotions paint the picture of Virgil's fall to the Shadow Lord.

She let the images wash through her, piecing them together, feeling her own emotions become pained and disheartened as Simon's feelings wove their threads through hers. Tears stung at her eyes, and she broke their connection so she could wipe them away with the back of her hand.

"How did it happen?" she asked, her tears spilling over even more. "How did they get him?"

"I don't know," Simon whispered, shaking his head slowly. "I have a guess, but...I don't know."

"Well," Abby said, sniffling and working to regain her composure, "we're just going to have to find a way to save him."

Simon nodded his agreement. "I've been thinking about that since I texted you. I think...I have an idea."

She frowned across the table. "Then why do you look so defeated?" she asked pointedly.

Simon looked up and met her eyes with his. "Because I don't really expect it to work," he said. "And if it doesn't..." He squirmed uncomfortably in his booth. "If it doesn't, I think it'll be bad. For Virgil."

Abby arched an eyebrow. "How bad?"

But Simon didn't have to respond. The grim, pale look on his face said it all.

"Oh," Abby said quietly, looking down at the table. "I see."

They sat in silence for several long minutes, lost in their own thoughts. They sipped from their coffees, and the waitress came over once to fill them. She asked if they wanted any food, but they shook their heads wordlessly. She walked away.

The café was quiet at this time of night. It was a twenty-four-hour restaurant, but situated close to downtown, and it didn't get much business after midnight during the week, which was why Simon had chosen it for his meeting with Abby. It wasn't a place he regularly went, so he didn't think Virgil would come looking for him there...and if he did, with the space being so empty, Simon would be able to see him coming.

He couldn't believe he now lived in a world where he was so terrified of his best friend.

"I need you to leave town," Simon said, breaking the silence. "Virgil's unhinged, and he wants to impress the Shadow

Lord to try to spare his own life. He'll come after me, but he'll come after you, too, I think. And Llewyn. It'll be easy for him, since Llewyn's still so weak."

"What about Morgaine?" Abby asked.

Simon shook his head. "For all we know, she'll throw in with the Shadow Lord if she gets the chance. Llewyn doesn't trust her, and he told us not to, either. If she realizes how much power the Shadow Lord has, she might fight to stop him, but she also might side with him and help him take over Templar. We can't ask her for help."

Abby nodded slowly, but she was frowning. "How long do I need to be gone?" she asked.

"I don't know," Simon admitted. "If I can take care of this tonight, then you can come back tomorrow."

"Tonight?" Abby said, alarmed. "Simon, you are *not* in any condition to take on Virgil *tonight!* Have you looked in a mirror?"

"It can't wait," Simon insisted. "If I can do it, you'll be safe tomorrow. But if Virgil—" A lump caught in Simon's throat. He swallowed it down. "If I can't stop him, then it might not be safe for a long time. At least until Llewyn is strong again. Maybe longer."

"So you want me to just abandon you both?" Abby snorted, and she crossed her arms in firm defiance. "Not a chance."

But Simon shook his head. "No. I want you to take Llewyn with you. You have to get him out of town, too. I want you to head back to his mansion tonight, right now. Make sure he's okay, then I want you to tear down the tent, fold it up, throw it into your truck, and get moving. Find some hotel across state lines and hole up for the rest of the night."

"The mansion won't collapse when I take down the tent?"

Simon shook his head. "The tent isn't the mansion, it's just the entrance. Take it down and get it out of town. As long as

Virgil doesn't know where to find you, he won't know where to find the tent, and Llewyn will be safe." Suddenly, Simon remembered the new entrance that Morgaine had unzipped through the Dark Matter office, and he groaned. "One other thing," he said. "If Morgaine is there, ask her to close up the back door. She'll know what you mean."

Abby eyed him suspiciously. "Okaaay..." she said.

Simon didn't have the time or the energy to explain any further. Maybe, just maybe, he thought, the connection between the office and the mansion would crumple when the tent did.

He reached out and squeezed Abby's hand. "Please, just trust me on this. And keep Llewyn safe."

"What if Morgaine's in the mansion?" she asked.

"Then take her, too. Fold up the tent with both of them inside. Getting her out of town will be good. Like pulling a wild card out of a deck."

Abby set her lips into a hard line as she considered Simon's bruises. "I don't like this," she stated for the record.

"I don't either."

Now it was Abby's turn to shift uncomfortably in her seat. "You don't even know where Virgil went. I doubt he's in the subway tunnel waiting for you, and I'm pretty sure he didn't go home."

Simon tapped his thumb against the rim of his coffee mug. "No," he confirmed. "He didn't. I went home for the car, and he wasn't there. But I have a pretty good idea where to find him." He checked the clock on his phone. It was getting close to one in the morning. "I'll call you. Before noon. To tell you it's safe to come back."

Abby sighed. "And if I don't hear from you?" she asked.

Simon exhaled and shook his head. He looked up at her, his blue eyes as cold as ice. "Then don't come back," he said.

They sat together for a few more minutes, holding one another's hands and letting the silence speak for them both. Then Abby got up, threw a few bills on the counter, and walked out the door without saying goodbye. She jumped in her truck and drove off toward the Mallard Street Bridge.

Simon watched her taillights disappear into the darkness. Then he threw down a few dollars of his own, pulled on his jacket, and headed out into the parking lot.

He had one quick stop to make. Then he was going to find Virgil.

CHAPTER 35

The fog was thick, and the night was dark, and Simon couldn't see Grimsley Manor until he was right at the edge of the clearing.

A fair number of lights burned within the old house, despite the late hour, casting warm, rosy glows through windows that were framed by dark stone walls, giving an uneven sort of shape to a mansion that stood silently in the near-total darkness of the cold autumn night. The overall effect sent chills through Simon's bones, even more than the damp air did.

Silhouettes passed in front of some of the windows, members of the shadow army moving quickly within the stolen house, and Simon realized that the manor must have been full of tension. By now, Virgil had spread the word of the closed portal to the Shadow Realm, and they all knew that their master was temporarily trapped in his own dimension. Simon could almost see the agitation in the silhouettes as they crisscrossed the hallways of the house, flitting from one window to the next, moving with jerky, excited, overly-animated motion.

It was proof enough for Simon that Virgil actually *was* inside, that he had returned to Grimsley Manor, just as Simon suspected. There wasn't anywhere else for him to go, really. Simon had checked both the apartment and the Dark Matter office, and had found them both empty. He was also relieved to see the back wall of the office zipped up again. Abby had texted to say that she had made it to Llewyn's and had passed the message about the back door to Morgaine. There was no sign of Virgil at the house, so Abby had walked back out of the tent, pulled it down from the rebar, folded up the canvas, and stuffed it into the back of her truck. By now, Simon surmised, she was almost to the West Virginia border.

Virgil was nowhere to be seen. Which meant he had returned home.

Or, at least, to what passed for his home now.

To what passed for his family now.

Simon felt his blood run hotly to his cheeks, and he worked to push down his anger. He needed a clear head if he was going to face Evil Virgil, and he didn't want his instincts clouded by emotion. Besides, the pumping blood made his jaw throb painfully. He had bought some ice at the QuikTrip, which had helped the swelling a bit. But his jaw was still sore, and it bore a nasty bruise.

He took a few deep breaths, and he felt his heart slow. He reached up and pulled down the ski mask so that it covered his face, and he prayed that, cloaked in black as he was, he would be invisible in the darkness.

He picked up the gas can and stepped out of the fog, into the clearing before Grimsley Manor. The darkness made his progress slow and clumsy, and it was difficult to tell how precisely the gasoline was splashing out of the can. It didn't have to be perfect, but it had to be good enough that Virgil would get the message.

The sharp, acrid stench of the gas filled his nostrils and burned his eyes, but he pressed on, pouring out the fuel in what he hoped were more or less orderly lines.

He couldn't face Virgil at the manor. Fighting Virgil there meant fighting an entire army, at least some of whom had surgically-implanted magical powers. As far as Simon could figure, there were three types of soldiers in the Shadow Lord's army:

There were the ones without shadows, like Virgil...those were the people who had been lured into the Shadow Realm, and who had been infiltrated and commandeered by their own shadows.

There were the elderly people who had drained Templar's teenagers of their youth; they were the ones who wore the purple robes, and they were loyal to the Shadow Lord for restoring their vitality and strength, for returning them to the primes of their lives.

And then there were the ones who were like Neil Grunberg, who hadn't lost his shadow, but who was loyal to the Shadow Lord without being forcibly taken over, for who-knew-what reason. In Neil's case, it seemed to be a thirst for evil sorcery and power. Maybe that was true for all of them.

Simon couldn't decide which type of soldier was the most dangerous. Any of them could walk freely among the people of Templar and not raise any flags. Even the ones without shadows could probably blend in easily on even the sunniest day, because how often did people pay attention to other people's shadows?

And all of them, no matter who they were, or how they came to the Shadow Lord, could be outfitted with magical powers, thanks to the surgeons and their glowing, magical stones.

Simon didn't feel particularly good about going up against any of them. He didn't feel good about going up against Virgil, either, but he didn't have a choice. If he didn't stop Virgil, then Virgil would kill him, and he would probably hunt down Abby and kill her, too, to prove how loyal he was to the Shadow Lord. Simon had to put an end to Virgil's evil aims, or die trying. He didn't know if he could pull off his plan, but he knew he could at least lessen his chances of failure by getting Virgil alone and facing him one-on-one.

And to do that, he'd have to draw him out of the mansion, far away from his fellow soldiers and onto neutral ground.

Simon shook out the last drops of gasoline onto the grass. He stepped back into the curtain of dense fog, careful to walk around his work. Once he was hidden in the mist, he pulled the ski mask off his head and draped it over the empty gas can. He turned back to the manor. "Let's finish this," he murmured.

He lifted his hand and shot an energy blast into the clearing. The heat of it sparked the lines of gasoline, and they roared to life, spelling out huge letters of flame against the backdrop of the dark, damp grass.

Simon walked back to his car, letting the fire rage behind him.

He was pretty sure Virgil would get the message.

CHAPTER 36

The city was quiet and dark. Templar seemed to be holding its breath.

Simon closed his eyes and let the silence work through him, calming his heartrate and soothing his fraying nerves.

Until that silence was broken by the sound of Virgil's voice.

"You basically burned down the mountain," he said.

Simon's hands clenched. He took a deep breath.

Then he opened his eyes and turned to face the shadow that controlled his friend.

"A mansion full of wizards, and we still had to put out the fire the old-fashioned way," Virgil continued, emerging from the darkness across the street. He ducked beneath the line of yellow tape and stepped into the parking lot, looking around at the rubble that filled the block—chunks of concrete, broken cinder blocks, steel beams, shards of brightly-colored plastic, and bits of neon light tubing, all strewn across the blacktop. "Squeezy Cheez has seen better days," he pointed out.

The Refracticore's lightning column had been harder on Squeezy Cheez than on the other places it had struck. Not only had it shot down through the ceiling and blown a hole through the roof, but it had also cut across the room, slicing a wide, ragged crease in the building. It had also gone the extra mile to cave in part of the structure, blocking Simon and Virgil from reaching the football player who it ultimately destroyed. What was left of the building after the elderly shadow soldiers had their fill and the energy column disappeared was a collapsing, decimated structure that wouldn't stand on its own for much longer. Demolition crews had come in earlier that week and started tearing down the whole building. They had pulled down all the walls, but they hadn't yet gotten around to clearing away the rubble.

"I thought you'd appreciate the gesture," Simon called down from his perch atop a wide, uneven concrete platform. He was standing just about where the prize counter had been before the destruction.

"You see the Nerf gun anywhere?" Virgil asked hopefully.

"Nope," Simon replied. "They cleared out the prizes."

Virgil sighed with disappointment. "That's too bad," he said. He slid his eyes over the wreckage. "I hope they rebuild. I loved this place."

"No you didn't," Simon said evenly.

Virgil grunted. "Well, no...not *me*," the shadow admitted. He gestured to the body he was wearing. "But, you know. 'Me.'"

He stopped at the base of the rubble, looking up at Simon with interest. "Well. You left me a message in fire that said, 'Squeezy Cheez,' which, I admit, looked pretty cool. And here I am." He spread his arms wide, as if he were about to take a bow. "Though if you really wanted to die this badly, you should have just let me kill you in the subway. I could be sleeping right now."

"This ends tonight," was all Simon said.

Virgil nodded solemnly. "I get it, I get it. Take the fight to me, don't give me time to plan, don't give me a chance to find Abby and cut her head off, or to take out Llewyn while he's weak. Is that the plan?"

Simon flushed with hot anger, but he was determined not to let Virgil get under his skin. "Pretty much," he replied, holding his tongue.

"But you're weak just now," Virgil continued, grinning up at Simon. "Tired, worn out, probably in a lot of pain. You don't need to tell me that I pack quite a punch." He held up his fist and admired it in the glow of the streetlights. "You're operating at half-capacity, tops."

"More than enough to stop a shadow who talks too much," Simon said, gritting his teeth.

"Maybe," Virgil admitted, shrugging carelessly. "Which is why I didn't come alone."

He gave a sharp whistle, and two figures emerged from the shadows across the street: a man from the left, and a woman from the right. They each wore purple cloaks with the hoods pulled up over their heads, marking them as former elderlies who had regained their youth from the innocent high-schoolers of Templar.

Simon could see that they'd been modified; the man's hands glowed purple beneath the sleeves of his robe, and the woman's eyes were bright green lights under her hood.

They advanced toward the rubble pile, hemming him in on either side.

"The real Virgil was brave enough to do his own dirty work," Simon called down to the shadow that controlled his friend.

"And look where that got him," Virgil sneered gleefully.

"Is that what happened?" Simon asked, stalling for time. He reached into his pocket and slowly took out his phone. "He went in after the Shadow Lord on his own?"

"As a matter of fact, would you believe it was pure luck?" Virgil said, his lips curling into a smirk. "He was on one of his subway joy rides, just rolling around the city. But he got on the wrong train. Or the right train, depending on your perspective."

"So that's how the Shadow Lord's been building up his army so quickly," Simon said. He woke up his phone and thumbed through his texts. "He switches the tracks and sends entire trains into the Shadow Realm."

"They slice 'em and stuff 'em," Virgil agreed, nodding, "then they send them back to this world."

Simon frowned, suddenly heavy with sadness. The fact that Virgil had been taken by pure chance...it was somehow worse than him being targeted on purpose. But he pushed the sadness down, working hard to keep his head clear. "Guess that's not something that'll be happening again for a while, though, huh? Now that the portal is closed and all."

Virgil gritted his teeth. He didn't respond. Instead, he glanced over at the woman in the purple robe and gave her a quick nod.

The woman held her hands up on either side of her face, and the light glowed brighter. With a loud cry, she shot a green laser blast from her eyes. The beam caught the rubble on the concrete platform beneath Simon's feet, slicing it in half. Simon leapt off the platform and landed unevenly on a twisted pile of metal. He threw up a kinesthetic shield as the laser beam swept over him. The shield absorbed the blast easily; the surgical magic wasn't quite as powerful as his natural paranormal energy...though given enough time, it would certainly wear him down enough for Virgil to easily finish him off.

Simon sensed movement over his shoulder and turned his head to see the man sneaking up behind him, charging up the purple light in his hands. Simon put his phone into his mouth to free up his other hand, and he fired a kinesthetic blast from his manacle. Simon had no interest in hurting Virgil's lackeys; his shot went purposely wide, exploding against the asphalt about eight inches to the man's left. It was close enough to make him dive behind a construction dumpster for cover.

The woman blinked and drew down her power. The green laser evaporated. Simon could see her breathing hard, already tired from her attack.

Virgil hadn't brought his A-team. He'd brought a couple of soldiers he considered expendable.

The cruelty of it made the hairs on the back of Simon's neck prickle up. But again, he pushed down his emotions, stuffing them down into his gut. Simon took the phone from between his teeth. "I had Abby send me a picture of something." He held it out to Virgil. "Not sure if you can see it from there."

Virgil squinted up at the phone, but he couldn't make out the image from so far away. "Okay, I'll bite. What is it?" he asked.

"It's a page from one of Llewyn's books." He crouched down amid the spires of twisted metal, which gave him an extra barrier against magic attacks from Virgil's foot soldiers, and he set the phone down on the rubble before him. "I only know a little Latin, but Abby promised me it was the right spell."

That got Virgil's attention. "What spell?" he asked, his spine stiffening. His fingers began to twitch nervously, and Simon could see that Virgil was sending thin streams of magic into his manacle, preparing himself for an attack.

Simon smiled. It felt good to have the upper hand on the shadow, even if only for a few seconds.

He closed his eyes and focused his thoughts, and when he opened them again, he was holding a multifaceted purple gemstone that was about the size and shape of a football. The light from the streetlamps flashed gold across its surface. "I'm getting pretty quick with my psychic vault," Simon said, allowing himself a moment of pride. "And it turns out, the Refracticore has a reverse setting."

Suddenly alarmed, Virgil charged up his manacle and fired a shot at Simon. But the magic blast hit one of the metal braces that coiled up around him, and Simon didn't even bother putting up a shield. He held the Refracticore in both hands, cradling it gently, and he began to recite the words on the page that Abby had texted him before folding up the tent and heading out of town. The first page that detailed the Refracticore, the one that Virgil had found open on Llewyn's desk after Llewyn had turned himself into a living icicle, had been written in glyphs that, as Virgil himself had noted, looked like squares and picnic tables. But the next page—the one that Virgil hadn't been able to turn because everything in the mansion had been frozen by then—showed the glyphs translated into Latin.

And Latin was a language that Simon could fake.

He mouthed the words of the spell, whispering them to the amethyst stone, and it began to glow with golden light at its core. Virgil threw another kinesthetic shot at the mountain of rubble, but that one went even wider, missing Simon by almost a whole foot.

Virgil was getting anxious, and it was making him careless.

He continued with the spell, saying the words and feeling fairly confident that he was pronouncing them correctly. If he could weave a Latin protection spell that could keep Asag at bay, he reasoned, he could surely manage a more than passable Refracticore incantation.

He finished the spell with a loud whisper of *"magicae retro reflectat,"* and he hoisted the Refracticore into the air. It burned with a shimmering gold light that glowed brighter and brighter at its core. Then it shot out a lightning bolt on either side. One caught the woman with the green eyes squarely in the chest; the other struck the man with the purple hands somewhere below his sternum. Both of the Shadow Lord's acolytes froze in place, their limbs stiffening, and their bodies lifting into the air. They hovered a few inches off the ground as bright white light shot out of their eyes and from the tips of their fingers.

The Refracticore stone did its terrible work, draining the stolen youth from the two shadow soldiers, and even though he expected it, Simon was still thrown by the extreme transformation as the people in the purple cloaks withered and shriveled into their proper forms. Even with their hoods drawn, Simon could see the skin of their hands and their cheeks wrinkle and tighten, and thin tufts of hair floating down from their hoods like grotesque snowflakes.

Then the Refracticore pulled in its bolts, drawing the youth-energy of the two shadow soldiers into itself, and the soldiers fell back onto the ground. Their knees buckled as their own bones betrayed them, cracking and popping beneath the shock of the impact against the asphalt. They writhed on the blacktop; the man tried to shoot a power blast up toward Simon, but his strength had been sapped, and the magic bolt came out as a weak fountain, spilling out of his palm and pooling in a puddle of light not three feet from where he lay.

Simon closed his eyes and accessed his psychic vault once more. In his mind, he placed the Refracticore back onto its shelf, then he closed the door of the vault, locked it, and opened his eyes.

"Guess it's just us now," he said, standing up from the rubble and giving Virgil a smirk.

Virgil ground his teeth so hard that Simon could hear the squeak of it from his perch. "I'll kill you for that," Virgil seethed, both of his hands glowing orange with kinesthetic rage.

He launched himself into the air, and the true battle began.

CHAPTER 37

Virgil swung down with a glowing orange fist, aiming for the swollen side of Simon's jaw. Simon ducked out of the way, and Virgil's fist slammed through the rubble, cracking holes in concrete and steel. He whipped his head around and glared at Simon. "Hold still," he sneered.

Virgil ripped his hand free of the debris as Simon rolled away, dodging through the twisted metal and skidding down a slope of ruined concrete. Virgil jumped down after him, shooting an orange blast at his head, but Simon deflected it easily with a shield. Then he twisted and swung the shield backward, catching Virgil in the jaw with the hard edge of the kinesthetic barrier and knocking him backward onto the ruins of the Squeezy Cheez.

"Let Virgil go!" Simon hollered up at the fallen form of his former friend.

The creature that presented himself as Virgil Matter raised his head. He grinned down at Simon, a thin trickle of blood running out from the corner of his mouth. "Not a chance," he replied.

Simon flushed with anger. He sent streams of kinesthetic magic into his left foot, then he stomped on the pile of rubble beneath him. A crack opened up in the concrete, splitting and spreading toward Virgil, opening up beneath him like a canyon. Virgil cried out in surprise as he fell into the shallow ravine, his hands flailing with frustration as he worked to claw his way out.

"There's no point!" Virgil screamed, struggling to pull himself up from the crack in the pile of debris. "Whatever you do to me, you do to Virgil! Maim me, and you maim him! And if you main him," Virgil seethed, pulling himself to his feet and stalking toward Simon, "I promise you, I will vacate his body in an instant and leave him to rot in the agony of it."

Simon took a deep breath and steeled himself against those words. He had no doubt that they were true. Virgil's shadow could live outside of Virgil's body; he'd seen the Shadow Lord slither around as nothing more than a loose shadow—in fact, he'd *only* seen the Shadow Lord in that form. Simon had to play his hand carefully. As much as he wanted the shadow to leave Virgil's body, it wasn't worth leaving Virgil as a desiccated mound of flesh and bone.

"Leave Virgil behind right now and I'll let you walk away," Simon promised, trying to keep his voice even. His heart was hammering in his chest, and adrenaline was surging through his veins. But he worked hard to keep himself even, to come across as a voice of reason to the shadow who lived inside his friend.

"You embarrass yourself by even asking," Virgil replied, glaring at Simon. "We both know that I'm stronger than you. But if you want to test it out, I'm happy to oblige."

Virgil shot a magic beam at Simon, who ducked out of the way just in time. The energy blast exploded on a chunk of cement just over Simon's shoulder. Virgil fired another attack, this one a series of fist-sized orange bombs that sailed through the air, peppering the ground around Simon. Simon threw up his hands and formed a shield that curved down around him, settling over him like a bubble, sealing him off from the hailstorm of magical missiles. The shield blinked in and out of being as the explosions wracked the kinesthetic barrier, but it held long enough for Simon to seize on a break in the volley.

He let the shield evaporate and dove to his left, hitting the rubble hard behind a heavy pile of bricks and scraping his elbow on the rough cement. He sucked in a pained breath through his teeth and rubbed the burn out of his arm.

He peeked his head up over the brick pile and nearly had it taken off by a magic blast. He ducked just in time, and the edge of the blast caught the top row of bricks, exploding them into shards that rained down on him from above.

Simon lunged to the side, peeking out from behind his barrier, and fired a shot from his manacle. It wasn't meant to hit Virgil, just to get close enough to throw him off balance, but as Virgil watched it streak toward him, he slammed the heels of his hands together and cast a refraction spell. The whole thing happened in an instant. Small flecks of blue energy flowed toward his hands, forming a blue lightning ball; Virgil cast the refraction, and the air in front of him shattered into a broken pane of reality just in time to catch Simon's magic blast. The orange streak disappeared into the refraction, which turned it around and shot it back out at Simon from six different directions at once. Simon cried out in alarm and dove back behind the bricks. A few of the blasts struck the barrier, and one shot down from above and singed Simon's right leg, just above his knee.

He clamped his teeth down and squeezed his eyes shut, biting back the pain.

He refused to give Virgil the satisfaction of hearing him scream.

The burn in his leg was deep. The refracted blast had carved a channel in the side of his thigh, but it had also cauterized the wound instantly, and there was no blood. Simon flexed his leg a few times, wincing at the tightness of his skin and the pain that shot through his leg when he moved it.

"You all right over there?" Virgil called out. Simon could hear rubble sliding and crumbling away as Virgil made his way closer to his hiding spot. Simon sent streams of magic down his arm and whispered a spell into his palm. A set of small, ember-orange beads formed in his hand. He launched them over his shoulder, lobbing them blindly toward Virgil. The beads exploded in the air, one by one, popping off a lout *RAT-TAT-TAT-TAT-TAT* as they detonated like flash-bang grenades, shooting out bright bursts of light around Virgil's head. Virgil cried out and threw his arms over his eyes, but the spell had done its work. The flashes had shocked his retinas and washed out his vision with a violent after-glare.

"Oh, *come on!*" Virgil shrieked, rubbing at his eyes. He blinked hard, trying to clear the glare. "Where did you even *learn* that?"

Simon seized his opportunity. He leapt over the brick wall, his leg screaming in pain. He threw open his left hand, and five kinesthetic threads shot out from his wrist. They caught Virgil as he stumbled across the concrete, wrapping up tightly around his ankles, cinching together his knees, then pulling tight against his shoulders and pinning his arms to his side as they tightened around his waist. Virgil yelled in anger and frustration, straining blindly at his bonds, but Simon's magic held tight. Virgil wrenched forward, and he lost his footing, crashing down onto the shards of brick and metal.

"Let me go!" Virgil screeched. The after-glare still blocked his vision, and he writhed angrily and painfully on the mountain of rubble. "Stop him! *Stop him!*" he screamed down at the elderly soldiers down on the pavement, but their strength and their will had left them, and they lay pitifully on the blacktop.

Simon took a deep breath and tried to steel himself for what he had to do. This was his chance, and if he hesitated, he might miss his only window. Virgil was incapacitated, but he wouldn't be for long; the power of the shadow inside him was strong, and once his vision cleared and his confusion subsided, he would make short work of the magical ropes.

And he wasn't likely to let himself be captured again.

It was now or never.

Simon knelt down next to Virgil, placed a hand on his shoulder, and spoke softly, despite Virgil's furious struggle. "I don't know what this is going to do to you, Virgil," he said quietly, swallowing back the lump that threatened to rise in his throat. "I know you don't want to live with the shadow inside you, and this is the only thing I can think to do."

Virgil snarled, snapping his teeth like a rabid animal. His vision began to clear, and his eyes focused on Simon. He let out a string of curses and tried to bite Simon's hand.

"I'm sorry, Virg," Simon whispered, squeezing his friend's shoulder. "I know you're in there, and I'm sorry. If this doesn't..." He took a deep breath and tried to re-center. "If this goes badly...I want you to know that you were a good friend. More than a good friend. You've been the family I didn't get to have."

He rubbed his nose with his sleeve, clearing away what was starting to drip. Tears dropped from his eyes, splashing on the dusty chunks of concrete. He closed his right hand into a fist, and when he opened it, one of the flash-bang beads sat in his palm.

He reached down with his left hand and gripped Virgil's jaw. He pushed his cheeks in and wrenched his mouth open. Virgil kicked and fussed, trying to pull free, but Simon held him tightly. "Light is the maker and the master of shadow," he whispered.

He jammed the flash-bang into Virgil's mouth and slammed his jaw closed. He held Virgil's head, pulling back against his struggles, keeping his mouth clamped shut.

Then the bead detonated, blasting the inside of Virgil with an explosion of searing white light. It flashed so brightly that Simon could see Virgil's skeleton through his skin. The light shot through every bit of him, blasting out through his eyes, his nostrils, his mouth, and his fingertips. The shadow inside of Virgil screamed as the light tore through him, ripping him to shreds, disintegrating him completely.

As soon as it flashed, the light subsided again, and Virgil fell quiet, his body going limp beneath the orange ropes of Simon's magic. Simon waved his hand over the bonds, and they disappeared.

Virgil's limbs were freed.

They fell against the rubble, lifeless and limp.

Simon looked down at his friend's body, and he trembled with fear. "Virgil?" he whispered, his voice catching in his throat. He gave Virgil a shake; Virgil did not respond. "Virgil?!" He shook him harder, trying to will him to life.

But there was no life left.

"*Virgil!*"

Simon put his hands on Virgil's chest, searching for a heartbeat, feeling nothing but stillness. He turned Virgil's wrist over, pressing his fingers against the veins and looking for a pulse that wasn't there.

Simon grabbed for his cell phone, his breath coming in shallow, labored gasps. He called 911 and babbled unintelligibly to the operator, screaming words into the phone that he wouldn't be able to recall later. Time came in waves, moving slowly, flashing forward, obscured by a numbness that deadened his every nerve.

By the time the ambulance lights flashed into the parking lot, Simon had collapsed onto the bricks and the dust, pinned down by the realization that Virgil was dead.

EPILOGUE

"Are you his family?"

Simon looked up, blinking in the harsh glare of the hospital's fluorescent lights. The doctor stood over him, glancing down nervously, tapping his thumbs against the clipboard in his hands.

The words reached Simon slowly, as if they were moving through water. "Family?" he asked slowly, trying to unstick his mind from the veil of Virgil's death that had closed across his brain. "I...sort of."

The doctor frowned. He glanced uneasily around the room, but there was no one else hovering over Virgil's body, or perched on the windowsill, or waiting nervously by the door. There was no one.

There was only Simon.

The doctor nodded. "Can we step outside?" he asked.

He helped Simon up to his feet and guided him out into the hallway. Orderlies rushed by with carts, and nurses stepped quickly from one room to the next. The doctor led Simon to an alcove near the door, helping him down onto one of the padded benches that ran along the inlet of the wall.

The doctor glanced at Simon uneasily, fiddling with his own fingers, shifting uncomfortably on his bench.

Finally, he cleared his throat. "Virgil..." he said. His voice caught. So he swallowed and tried again. "Virgil is in a coma."

Simon's eyes lifted. They were swollen and red, ringed with dark pouches. "A coma?" he repeated, confused.

The doctor breathed a heavy sigh. "It's bad," he said. "I'm sorry. It's my job to tell you. It's bad."

Simon furrowed his brow. "A coma?" he said again, staring quizzically at the doctor.

The doctor nodded. "I know it's not what you want to hear..." he began.

"He's not dead?" Simon asked. His voice was squeaky and high, strung tight with absolute astonishment.

The doctor looked at him, confused. "Dead?" he asked, planting his hands on his knees and leaning forward with curiosity. "No, he's...he's not dead."

Simon's eyes grew wide. He bolted up from his seat on the bench "He's *alive?*"

The doctor was taken aback. He raised his hands and waved them in the air, as if trying to tamp down Simon's expectations. "Well, yes, but...you understand what a coma is, yes?"

Simon's mouth hung open. He sputtered a serious of unintelligible sounds before finding his words. "He wasn't breathing when he—when I—when they took him!" he said.

"That can happen," the doctor replied, nodding mournfully. He leaned forward, his hands still firmly on his knees. "I know this must sound like relief, then, but I have to tell you, it's still not good news," the doctor cautioned, his brow creased with worry.

"But he's alive!" Simon shouted. A few of the nurses out in the hall glanced in his direction, thrown by the sudden shout from across the hall. Simon didn't notice. "He's alive!" he shouted again.

The doctor nodded, but he gestured for Simon to return to his seat on the bench. "He is, but...you have to understand something important." The doctor leaned forward and chose his words carefully. "Virgil is in what is called a complex coma."

"What's a complex coma?" Simon asked, his excitement slowly deflating. He felt a familiar ball of dread clench in the pit of his stomach.

"Well...I'm not sure, exactly," the doctor admitted, looking troubled. "What I mean is, his vital signs are unusual for a coma patient. Most show *very* little brain activity, but Virgil's brain is *extremely* active. I would go so far as to say frantic."

Simon frowned. "Frantic?" he said.

The doctor nodded solemnly. "Virgil's brain currently shows more activity than the average conscious person." He took a deep breath before sitting back in his chair and throwing up his hands. "To be frank, I've never seen anything like it. He should be awake, but he's not. It's like he's…I don't know, it's like he's *here*, but also…not. I'd liken it to *encephalitis lethargica*—are you familiar?" Simon shook his head, and the doctor continued. "It's sometimes called sleeping sickness. Virgil's case shares symptoms, but this is different and is more severe in several ways. Like his…I don't know, this isn't my field, I feel strange even saying it, but—" He hesitated, and he looked as if he were trying to decide whether to keep going with his thought.

"But what?" Simon prodded.

The doctor sighed. "I have a colleague who practices—well, let's say, a different sort of medicine. Eastern philosophy, mixed with South American mysticism." He held up his hands and shook his head as if to cut Simon off before he could voice his skepticism. "I know, I know. It's…well, if you ask me, it's nonsense. But I mention him because I once heard him describe a patient in a way that comes to mind now to describe Virgil. Which is that he seems almost as if…as if his consciousness is…*trapped*."

Simon bit his lip, trying to process what the doctor was saying. "Well…when do you think he'll come out of it?" he asked cautiously.

The doctor furrowed his brow. He looked genuinely pained. "Unfortunately, I think the question we should be asking is, *will* he come out of it at all? And I'm afraid I can't answer that."

"You're a doctor," Simon said, feeling a confusing mixture of anger and fear spread through his chest. "You're supposed to be the only one who *can* answer that!"

The doctor's watch buzzed, and he looked down at the screen. Then he slapped his thighs and stood up. "I have a patient," he explained. "We'll do everything we can."

He shook Simon's hand, but Simon barely registered the motion. His head was spinning; the room felt like it was short on oxygen, and the thought that he had done this to Virgil pierced his heart like an icicle.

The doctor patted him on the shoulder, then left him in the alcove. He had made it two steps into the hallway when he froze. He stopped in mid-step, with one bent leg lifted up into the air. And he just stood like that for several seconds, frozen in place.

"Doctor?" Simon asked cautiously. He stood up from the bench and approached the unmoving man. "Are you...okay?"

The doctor slowly lowered his leg. He stretched out his arms and looked down at them, inspecting them as if they were new. He made a similar inspection of the rest of his body, looking down his lab coat and turning to the side, admiring the sides of his shoes. Then he looked back over at Simon.

Simon gasped.

The doctor's eyes had changed color, from brown to a grayish-blue, and were filmed over with spinning, swirling clouds.

"So you're thinking this is pretty weird, right?" the doctor said. His voice had changed, too; it was no longer the slow baritone of the man who had spoken haltingly about Virgil's health. It was now a higher-pitched, windy sort of sound that was oddly familiar...

"Doctor?" Simon said again, backing slowly away from the changed man.

"Oh, on the outside, yeah," the doctor agreed, nodding enthusiastically. "Sorry, I know this is weird. I'm just borrowing him for a second. I had to talk to you, and if you don't fall asleep, you can't come to me, so I had to come to you, and this was the quickest way. It's a whole thing."

Simon stumbled backward onto his bench and plopped down onto his seat, stunned. "I...*know* you," he said slowly.

"Well, yeah...duh," the doctor said, rolling his cloudy gray eyes. "Usually I'm doing this." The doctor held his arms straight out at his sides and began to spin in circles, picking up speed as he went.

"You're the cyclone," Simon said, creasing his brow in confusion. "From the dark-sky place. From my dreams."

"Not *exactly* from your dreams," the doctor replied, still spinning like a top. "But yeah, basically. That's me. So, listen." The doctor slowed his spinning and came to a halt facing Simon. "Are you busy right now?"

"Are you...inside the doctor?" Simon asked, perplexed.

"Yeah. Look, I only have a few seconds, I can't take over people's bodies for very long. I came to tell you: I hope you're not busy right now, because you really need to get moving."

"Moving?" Simon asked. "Moving where?"

"Well, I don't know where to start, but I bet your wizard does," the doctor said. He began to spin in circles again, and the nurses at the desk behind him gave him strange looks. He stopped his twirling, holding up a hand to them in apology. "Sorry. Habit." He flashed them an awkward smile.

"What are you talking about?" Simon said, trying to wrap his brain around the fact that the cyclone from his dreams had possessed the body of Virgil's doctor. "You don't know where to start *what*?"

Now it was the doctor's turn to look confused. "Your journey to the Dark Below," he said, as if it were the most obvious thing in the world.

"The Dark Below?"

"Yeah. Look, Simon, I need you to focus here," the doctor said, snapping his fingers in front of Simon's nose. "We have to get you to the Dark Below—like, *now*. You're running out of time."

Simon shook his head slowly from side to side. "Running out of time to do *what*, exactly?" he asked.

"To save Virgil!" the cyclone cried.

Simon closed his eyes and rubbed his temples. He was so confused. "But Virgil's in there," he said, pointing in the direction of Virgil's room.

"No! Simon!" The doctor stepped forward and grabbed Simon by the shoulders, giving him a gentle shake. "That's not Virgil! Virgil is in the Dark Below! Don't you see?" His eyes filled with urgency as he searched for signs of comprehension.

"No..." Simon replied slowly.

"The Dark Below, Simon! Vampires and ash! You have to go to the Dark Below! Do you understand me?"

"No, I don't understand you!" Simon cried.

"You have to go to the Dark Below! *You have to save Virgil!*"

SIMON WILL RETURN IN:

THE DARK BELOW

BOOK FOUR OF
THE DARK MATTER SERIES

A NOTE FROM THE AUTHOR

If you enjoyed this book, please take a moment to leave a review on Amazon. Reviews really do make or break the success of a book for independent authors, and your support would be truly and greatly appreciated.

ABOUT THE AUTHOR

Clayton Smith is an award-winning Midwestern writer who once erroneously referred to himself as a "national treasure." He is the author of several novels, short story collections, and plays, including the best-selling Apocalypticon series. His short fiction has been featured in national literary journals, including Canyon Voices and Write City Magazine.

He is also rather tall.

Find him online StateOfClayton.com and on social media as @Claytonsaurus.

Made in the USA
Middletown, DE
28 July 2024

58110031R00119